Diamond Fire

By Ilona Andrews

Hidden Legacy series
BURN FOR ME
WHITE HOT
WILDFIRE
DIAMOND FIRE (novella)

Kate Daniels series
MAGIC BINDS
MAGIC GIFTS (novella)
MAGIC BREAKS
MAGIC RISES
MAGIC SLAYS
MAGIC BLEEDS
MAGIC STRIKES
MAGIC BURNS
MAGIC BITES

The Edge series
ON THE EDGE
BAYOU MOON
FATE'S EDGE
STEEL'S EDGE

Diamond Fire

A HIDDEN LEGACY NOVELLA

ILONA ANDREWS

AVONIMPULSE
An Imprint of HarperCollinsPublishers

DIAMOND FIRE. Copyright © 2018 by Ilona Gordon and Andrew Gordon. All rights reserved. Printed in the United States of America. No part of this book may be used or reproduced in any manner whatsoever without written permission except in the case of brief quotations embodied in critical articles and reviews. For information, address HarperCollins Publishers, 195 Broadway, New York, NY 10007.

Digital Edition NOVEMBER 2018 ISBN: 978-0-06-287841-0
Print Edition ISBN: 978-0-06-287843-4

Cover art by Gene Mollica

Avon Impulse and the Avon Impulse logo are registered trademarks of HarperCollins Publishers in the United States of America.
Avon and HarperCollins are registered trademarks of HarperCollins Publishers in the United States of America and other countries.

FIRST EDITION

18 19 20 21 22   HDC   10 9 8 7 6 5 4 3 2 1

Ramirez Family Tree

Mrs. Rogan's Siblings

Mattin, Inigo, Miren, Arrosa, Mirkel (half-brother), Ane (half-sister), Zorion (half-brother)

Guests of the West Wing

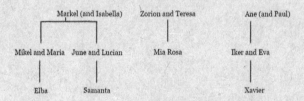

Paul and Isabella have no blood ties to the family.

Prologue

Nevada

ALL FAMILIES HAVE odd moments. Our family just has them more often than others.

I sat at our family kitchen table and stuffed my face with pancakes.

Arabella, my youngest sister, peered at me from across the table. "Why are you here? You don't even live here anymore, Nevada."

I had officially moved out yesterday. I'd spent the last nine years of my life in the second-floor suite of the warehouse that served as both our home and our business. Given that I now spent most of my time with Connor, otherwise known as Mad Rogan, and we recently became officially engaged, I decided to move out. There was surprisingly little fanfare. I hadn't accumulated much, and it took me less than a day to pack my belongings into boxes. Rogan's people got them last night and delivered them to his house, on the outskirts of Houston. Grandma Frida cried a little bit and Mom made a lot of grumpy noises, so I'd stayed the night in Rogan's HQ across the street just in case they decided to have a nervous breakdown about it.

I shouldn't have worried.

"Leave her alone," Mom told Arabella. "That's her third pancake."

"So?" Arabella glanced at me.

I stuck my tongue out at her and cut another piece of pancake with my fork.

"She's stress eating," Grandma Frida volunteered. "Rogan's picking her up in five minutes. She's scared to meet his mother."

Thank you, Grandma. I choked on my pancake and gulped my coffee. "I'm not scared."

I was totally scared. He'd wanted to take me to see her right after the trials, but I begged off for three days. There was no escape now. I had to meet my future mother-in-law.

Arabella squinted at me. Grandma Frida was past seventy and Arabella was still fifteen, but in that moment, they looked remarkably alike: both blue eyed, both pale haired—although Grandma Frida's curls were white because of her age—and both wearing identical sly expressions.

"You're wearing a pair of new jeans and your favorite green blouse," Arabella said.

"So?"

My sister dipped her blond head under the table. "And pretty, strappy sandals. And your toenails have polish."

"I can have polish on my toenails." Usually I wore sneakers because I occasionally needed to run in the course of my job, but I owned three pairs of sandals too.

"You better brush your teeth," Grandma Frida said. "You don't want coffee breath."

My toothbrush was at Rogan's HQ. Damn it.

"Stop it, the two of you," Mom growled and turned to me. "You'll be fine."

After Dad died, Mom became an unmovable rock in our turbulent sea. No matter what happened, she would be there, fixing it. It took me a long time to learn to look past that armor. The last year made that especially clear. But today I needed that rock and so I grabbed on to it.

"Mom says I'll be fine," I told them. "You've met her, Arabella. You could just tell me what she's like."

Arabella smiled. "I like watching you squirm."

My phone chimed. A text from Rogan. "You're missing the show."

"What show?"

"Come outside."

I really wanted to run upstairs to my old room and lock the door. I couldn't do that for two reasons. One, I was an adult, and two, my other sister, Catalina, moved into my room, so it wasn't technically mine anymore.

It was absurd. I was a trained private investigator with almost ten years of experience. Baylor Investigative Agency existed today because I took it over when Dad got sick and made it successful against all odds. Not only that, but I was a Prime, the highest level of magic user one could reach. My paternal grandmother had the same talent, and people cringed when they heard her name. I had stood up to her and to a dozen other Primes. In the past year I've been shot at, hit with a car, burned, teleported, and frozen nearly to death. I had a bus almost dropped on me, I faced a psionic who nearly destroyed my mind, and I told Connor Rogan, the Scourge of Mexico, "no" repeatedly and stood my ground. I should be able to meet my fiancé's mother.

I could do this.

I got up, put my plate into the sink, hugged my mom, and went to the door.

A gunmetal grey Range Rover waited in front of our warehouse. Unless you looked closely and knew what you were looking for, you would never guess that the car was armored.

Rogan leaned against the vehicle. I've seen him in a twenty-thousand-dollar suit and in dirt-stained jeans and a T-shirt. No matter what he wore, he always had a kind of rugged masculinity about him. You got a sense that nothing would knock him off his stride. Whatever came up, he would handle it and he wouldn't panic. The fact that he was huge—over six feet tall and built like he fought people for a living—only added to it. Today he wore a pair of jeans and an olive T-shirt. With his bronze skin and dark hair, he looked like some sort of jungle explorer.

Oh no.

I stopped.

"What?" he asked.

"We match," I ground out.

"So?"

"I'm going to go change."

He caught my hand and drew me to him. His dark blue eyes were laughing as he leaned down and kissed me. He tasted of mint and coffee and the touch of his lips anchored me. You know what, it would be fine.

"You look great. Also, if you leave, you'll miss the best part."

He nodded to my left. I glanced in that direction.

A sapphire-blue Maserati GranCabrio was parked at the curb. Next to it, directly under my—no, my sister's—window stood Alessandro Sagredo.

When I first saw Alessandro's picture shortly before the trials, I thought he looked like the son of a gladiator ready for his first match. That impression was even stronger in person. His face still had traces of softness, but they were quickly disappearing. The lines of his face were becoming hard and precise, but whichever form they would take, one thing remained certain—

Alessandro was cursed to spend his life being ridiculously handsome.

My shy quiet sister was leaning out of her window and seemed clearly agitated.

"No!" Catalina declared.

"Why not?" Alessandro's voice held just the slightest trace of an Italian accent.

"Because what you're feeling for me isn't real."

"Who says I'm feeling anything? I'm just suggesting we go for a drive." Alessandro nodded at the Maserati gleaming bright blue in the sunlight. "I have the car right here."

"No."

Only a few days ago, our family had to undergo the trials to prove that we possessed at least two Primes and therefore could be declared a House. We needed the protections granted to the emerging houses desperately, which meant that I and my sisters had to demonstrate our magical abilities before a panel of Prime judges. Alessandro was Catalina's test. A powerful Antistasi Prime, he could nullify others' magic, while my sister possessed the ability to make people love her. They had stood facing each other, with a white line between them. Then Catalina told him a story about our vacation in Florida and by the end of it, Alessandro crossed the line and fought the four people who tried to stop him. He'd shrugged it off in seconds, but my sister was declared a Prime.

"I thought Catalina's magic wore off with time," Rogan said quietly.

"It does. I don't think he's here because of her magic. He followed her on Instagram before the trials."

Rogan's dark eyebrows crept up a fraction of an inch. "And that's significant why?"

"He is a teenage heartthrob and Herald's darling with a couple million followers. He followed three people and Catalina. She became Instagram-famous overnight and deleted her account."

In our world Primes were the most prominent of celebrities. There was an entire social network dedicated to the obsession—the Herald, where members posted speculation, rumors, and fan fic. Alessandro Sagredo, being young, unmarried, and devastatingly handsome, was Prime groupie magnet, and Catalina hated attention of any sort. She had good reasons for it. I would've given anything to make it easier on her, but all magic came with a price and my sister had drawn the short stick.

"You need distance," Catalina declared. "It will wear off with time and distance."

Alessandro hung his head, his longish brown hair falling over his face. *"Per l'amor del cielo!"*

I turned to Rogan. "What did he say?"

"No clue."

"I'm not under the influence of your magic. I'm not climbing the walls to get to you. I'm just here to invite you to go for a quick drive."

A long pause ensued.

Alessandro tilted his head and gazed at the window.

Modern-day Romeo in luxury jeans next to his one-hundred-and-seventy-thousand-dollar steed.

Silence stretched.

"Is there going to be an answer?" Rogan asked me.

"No."

"She's just going to leave him standing there?"

"No, I meant that the answer will be no." I smiled at him. "Let's go. This is hard enough for Catalina as is, and we're not helping."

"I hate that window," Rogan said, as we got into his car.

Across the street, a heavy crate rose a few inches off the ground.

"Don't you dare," I told him. The memory of the last time we had an argument at that window was still fresh. Rogan was a Prime Telekinetic and he didn't like fighting with me from the street. He'd stacked half of the contents of his motor pool against the wall of our warehouse, so he could get to the window and talk to me face-to-face. "Seriously, this won't help."

The crate landed back on the pavement. Rogan drove out of the parking lot. "Poor count."

I glanced at him. "What do you mean?"

"Alessandro is a count. Conte di Sagredo. They date back to the twelfth century."

"Don't tell Catalina," I said.

My sister was self-conscious enough around regular people. Carrying on a conversation with someone who came from an old noble family would cause a complete shutdown. She would obsess over every word trying to make sure she didn't say something embarrassing or draw attention to herself.

It was enough that Alessandro was handsome, a Prime, and a verified teen heartthrob. Throwing a title in there would only make things worse.

THE LONG ROAD veered gently between rugged hills rising from the green cushion of ashe junipers and live oaks. We were climbing our way northwest, into Texas Hill Country. The ground looked dry, with big limestone boulders thrusting through the thin layer of topsoil. After the humidity of Houston, looking out of the car window made me thirsty.

"Why here?" I asked.

"She says the hills remind her of home," he said.

"Where is home?"

"Spain. Basque country, near Navarre, in the mountains. I've been there. It's not a perfect match, but it's dry and rugged in places, like here."

The road turned, and as Rogan smoothly took the curve, I saw the house. It crowned the hill, a beautiful Mediterranean mansion, its adobe walls interrupted by tall gleaming windows. We kept turning and the house kept going and going . . .

"What if she doesn't like me?"

"She will like you. I love you and that's all that really matters. But my mother will like you."

The road brought us to the apex of the hill, to a stone wall topped by a red clay roof. A sturdy metal gate guarded the entrance. It swung open at our approach and the Range Rover smoothly rolled down the long driveway, past the landscaped lawn to another arched entrance. We passed through it to the courtyard with a beautiful fountain in its center. Rogan brought the car to a stop.

"That's a giant house," I said.

"Mountain Rose. Twenty-two thousand square feet. Ten bedrooms. Twelve bathrooms. Two swimming pools. Tennis court, gardens, the works." Rogan grimaced. "I once asked my mother why she needed a house that large, and she said, 'For the grandchildren.'"

"You don't have any siblings, do you?"

"No." He moved his hand, indicating the length of the house. "One bedroom for her, one for us—that leaves eight bedrooms' worth of grandchildren, all on our shoulders."

"Great." It wasn't my shoulders I was worried about, but if I told him that, it would take him another ten minutes to get all of the funny innuendo out of his system.

We sat for a long moment. I didn't want to get out.

"Chicken?" he asked.

People lied every day, sometimes a dozen times a day, often for the best of reasons, but every time they bent the truth, my magic warned me. So I had long ago made it a point to lie as little as possible, and to Rogan not at all. He couldn't lie to me, and we had to come to this relationship as equals. "Yes."

"It will be fine." He reached over and kissed me. It was a quick kiss, meant to reassure, but about half a second into it, Rogan changed his mind. His hand caught my hair. He tasted like sandalwood, mint, and Connor. I sank into it and kissed him back. There was nothing like kissing Rogan. All my worries vanished and it was me and him, his taste, his smell, his touch . . .

We broke the kiss. His blue eyes turned darker. He looked like he was going to go in for seconds.

We couldn't just stay in the car making out. Arrosa Rogan was a Prime. She lived in a mansion with Prime-level security, which meant our kissing was likely splashed in horrifyingly HD detail on the internal security screens.

I opened my door. He grinned at me and we got out of the car.

The inside of the house was as impressive as the outside. The walls, covered with delicate swirls of beige and cream plaster, swept up to tall ceilings. The floor was travertine, laid in large slabs rather than typical tiles. The furniture had the same timeless quality as the pieces in Rogan's house, but where his furnishings were solid and almost plain, with a lot of square angles, the couches and chairs here were more ornate. There was something undeniably feminine about it.

Nobody came to greet us. Odd. Was this a power play of some kind? Was she putting me in my place by making me wait? All my nervousness came right back.

Rogan strode to the kitchen and opened the huge

fridge. I almost called to him to stop but caught myself. To me it was a mansion. To him it was his mother's house, and like any kid returning home, he made a bee-line for the fridge. I did the same thing when I walked through the door into the warehouse this morning.

"Would you like a drink?"

"What are my choices?"

"Sparkling water, iced tea, juice . . ."

"Tea. Thank you."

The kitchen was vast, with dark brown cabinets and beautiful granite countertops. State-of-the-art appliances waited to be used. The cooktop looked like something out of a kitchen competition show.

Rogan poured us two tall glasses of tea. I slid my butt onto a stool at the other end of the island and he pushed one glass toward me. I picked it up and drank.

Eight bedrooms' worth of grandchildren. Right.

I always wondered why Rogan was the only child. Primes warred with each other like medieval city states, and most Prime families took pains to ensure an heir and a spare. There was no spare. There was only Rogan. I've been meaning to ask him why but kept forgetting, and right now didn't seem to be the best time.

A mechanical whisper made me turn. A woman in a motorized wheelchair rolled into the kitchen. She was middle-aged and beautiful, with dark hair touched by grey, bottomless dark eyes, and bronze skin.

Oh.

Rogan walked over to her, leaned, and kissed her on the cheek. "Hi, Mom."

She smiled at him. They looked so alike.

"There is smoked brisket in the fridge," she said.

"I saw."

Arrosa turned to me. "Hello, dear."

"Hi." I remembered to get off the chair, took a few steps forward, and stopped, not sure what to do with myself.

"She's nervous, because you're scary," Rogan told her.

You traitor. I would remember this.

My future mother-in-law leaned her head back and laughed.

WE SAT UNDER the roof of a balcony on the second floor. Rogan had gone inside to make tea for his mother. The rain finally came, and the air felt crisp and cold.

"He didn't tell you about the chair, did he?" Arrosa asked.

"No."

She smiled. "Silly boy. It happened when he was three years old. His father was a target of an assassination. He was supposed to have been alone in a hotel room in New York, but I went with him. I'd had a bad feeling about that trip. He and I survived, which was all that mattered."

She got hurt trying to protect her husband. "I'm so sorry."

"I'm used to it. And my magic makes matters a lot easier. Are you cold?"

"I'm okay."

"You look cold. Here."

The big wooden chest on the side of the outdoor sofa opened and a blanket floated to me. Like Connor, Arrosa was a Prime Telekinetic.

"Thank you." I tucked the blanket around myself.

"Most men in Will's position would have divorced me. Connor was our only child. It was a risk to rely on only one heir to carry the line forward. But Will loved me very much and here we are."

"Rogan said that yours was an arranged marriage." I probably shouldn't have said that.

Arrosa's eyes sparkled. "He did, did he? Connor is very angry at my father. Yes, it started out that way. My family isn't a House. The bloodline frequently produces magic users of Significant and Average caliber, but my grandfather was a Prime. The family always hoped that another would be born and when I tested as a Prime, my relatives threw the biggest party. Hundreds of people were invited. My father, Rogan's grandfather, had great hopes for me. I was not to be married off; I would remain with the family; my spouse would join the family and take my name; and the two of us would be expected to have as many children as possible in hopes that we produced more Primes."

Made sense. I had looked up the Ramírez family. To be considered a House, they had to produce two Prime magic users in three generations. Arrosa's grandfather died before she was born, but if Arrosa had a child who tested as Prime, the Ramírez family could petition to become a House.

Arrosa pulled her shawl tight around her shoulders. "All those plans . . . And then Will Rogan showed up. My genetic profile matched his requirements and he traveled to Spain to meet me. I remember the first time I saw him. I was standing in the library, trying to sort the books, so I had several books floating over my head, and he was walking by and stopped in the doorway. We just stood and looked at each other. I had never seen anyone like him."

She smiled at the memories. I had a moment like that too. The first time I saw Connor, he was walking toward me through the park and I just sat there and watched him and wished that one day I could find someone like him.

"What happened?" I asked.

"My father told him no. Not many people told Will Rogan no. He was a third generation Prime. His magic was off the charts. He had military contracts, civilian contracts, foreign contracts, and half of the world owed him a favor. It is fair to say that in some respects Connor is a lot like his father."

In my experience, Connor acted as if the word no meant nothing unless he was the one saying it.

"Will made sure to run into me when I was in town. We talked. Then I met him again. And again. It was so easy talking to him. We were different, but it was effortless. So, he came to see my father again, and my father, who by that point realized that offending House Rogan wouldn't end well, told Will that he would have to compensate the family for the loss of a Prime. He named an outrageous amount of money. Will wrote the check on the spot. Nearly bankrupted himself." Arrosa's eyes narrowed and I saw a glimpse of power, sharp and frightening. Alarm shot through me.

"My father called me into his study and told me that Will bought me, and I had to go with him. And you know what my Will told him?"

"No."

"He said, 'Aren't you going to ask her if she wants to come with me? It's her decision.' And my father told him I would do what was best for the family. He didn't get it. He never did."

I was 100 percent with Rogan. I didn't like his grandfather either. "Did you ever regret it?"

"Never. Will was everything to me. We came home. His family wasn't thrilled that he signed away nearly three-quarters of his assets. His father once called me their Louisiana Purchase. It didn't matter. We worked together to rebuild what he had lost. We were a great team. He loved me, Nevada. I got to experience the kind of love very few people do. I miss him every day. Sometimes I wake, and I reach over, expecting him to be in bed with me. But he is never there. I do still talk to him. He is buried in the gardens, next to his parents."

This could be me. If I married Rogan, in a few years I could be sitting in her spot, mourning my husband. Primes swam in dangerous waters. It was almost enough to make you reconsider, but I wanted Connor too much. A week or fifty years, I would take whatever time we could have together.

"Do you love Connor?" Arrosa asked.

"Yes." It wasn't even a question.

"And what about children? You are probably not genetically compatible. Does that bother you?"

"I want to have his children. I will love them whether they have magic or not."

Arrosa's eyes narrowed again. "Connor, you, and your children will be in danger much more frequently than most people. You are Primes. We live by different rules and my son has made powerful enemies. Some women would take an easier path."

Okay, I didn't like what she was implying. I raised my head. "I may not be a telekinetic, but I promise you, anybody who thinks they can harm Connor or our children will have to go through me and they will change their mind fast. If they have a mind left by the time I'm done."

She scrutinized my face. "What if I decide that I don't like this marriage?"

My heart made a flip in my chest. I was afraid of that. "Then I'm very sorry. I have the deepest respect for you and I will still strive to be the best daughter-in-law I can be. But I love him, and I will marry him."

Connor chose that moment to walk out on the balcony, carrying a platter with three steaming coffee mugs filled with tea. "Are you done torturing Nevada?"

"I like her," Arrosa said.

What?

"How in the world did you manage to get her?"

"He kidnapped me and chained me to the floor in his basement."

"What?!"

"It was a misunderstanding," Rogan said and shot me a look. Yeah, payback is a bitch. Deal with it.

"I am going to need the whole story," Arrosa said.

"Does this mean you will attend the wedding?" he asked.

"What kind of a question is that?"

And my future husband just successfully derailed his mother's train of thought and sent her into a new direction. *Nice.*

Arrosa floated her cup to her and sipped. "Have you set a date?"

"In a couple of weeks," Connor said.

"Out of the question. It will take that long just to inform all of the family."

Family? What family? I glanced at Connor. "I thought you didn't have any family?"

"Oh, he does. He has a grandfather, four uncles, two aunts, fourteen cousins, some of them with their own children, and that's not counting the extended family. Most of them are from my side and they live in Spain. He just doesn't like some of them very much."

I pivoted to Connor.

"Some of them are vultures," he said and drank his tea. "I want a simple wedding, Mother."

"Connor Ander Rogan."

Oh-oh. Middle name. Never a good sign.

"I was planning to invite Uncle Inigo," he said. "And Uncle Mattin. What if we only invite the ones I like? If we're inviting everyone, perhaps we should invite Kelly."

Oh, that was a low blow. Kelly Waller was Connor's cousin and she and her son were the only surviving blood relatives from his father's side. In a family of magic users, she was born with a weak talent, while Connor's power was off the charts. She'd married for love instead of genetics, and her parents cut her off. From her point of view, she had lost everything. She and her husband struggled, and she had expected Connor, her baby cousin, to set things right when he became an adult. Instead Connor enlisted in the Army and went to fight his own war. She felt twice betrayed.

By the time he came back and tried to reach out, her jealousy and resentment had gone toxic. She hated him and the family so much she'd tried to kill Connor on multiple occasions. For this purpose, she gave her only son, Gavin, to a psychopathic Prime, who used him to murder an off-duty cop. Now Gavin sat in prison, and only Connor's influence and a great deal of investigative work on my end had kept him from being shot on sight.

We would probably invite Gavin and his father. I was reasonably sure that the Rogan family name would buy Gavin a day pass. Kelly was a fugitive, from both the law and the House Assembly. If I saw Kelly, I would put a bullet between her eyes without hesitation. I wouldn't try to apprehend her or talk to her. I would shoot her until I ran out of bullets.

Arrosa looked at him. "Is this a practice marriage for you? Are you planning on divorcing Nevada and doing this again?"

Rogan's face took on that look of intense concentration that usually meant he expected someone to shoot at us. "No."

Magic snapped out of my mother-in-law and I nearly fell out of my chair.

"You are my only son," Arrosa Rogan declared.

The loving mother had vanished. Her expression hardened, her eyes narrowed, and the tone of command in her voice made me want to snap to obey. She would give Grandma Victoria a run for her money.

"If fortune smiles on us, this will be your only wedding. This will be a formal affair. Your bride will be wearing a breathtaking gown, you will be wearing a tuxedo, and I will watch you two exchange vows and kiss in front of our entire family and all of our friends, and I will glow with pride at this moment. You will not rob me of that joy. Later I will talk to your father about it and tell him how beautiful it was. Am I making myself clear?"

The Scourge of Mexico and the most terrifying Prime in Houston unhinged his manly jaws and said the only thing he could, "Yes, Mother."

"Wonderful. We will set the date three months from now. That will give everyone time to rearrange their schedules." Arrosa turned back to me and smiled, all warmth and sunshine again. "I'm so excited! My dear, the dress, the hair, the flowers. You have so many wonderful decisions to make."

Chapter 1

Two months and two weeks later
Catalina

I FOUGHT MY way through the hallway of Mountain Rose house trying to dodge the children. Everything I ever read about my future brother-in-law on Herald suggested that Connor Rogan was a loner with no immediate family besides his mother and his cousin, Kelly Waller, who didn't count.

Herald lied.

The gaggle of children was coming right for me.

I clutched my tablet to my chest and braced myself.

They ran around me in circles, giggling, and dashed down the hallway, leaving a little girl holding a stuffed unicorn in their wake. I let out a breath.

Rogan had oodles of relatives, scattered all over the Mediterranean, and all of them descended on his mother's house to attend the wedding. I liked kids, but there were somewhere between twenty and thirty children under the age of twelve on the premises and they traveled in packs. The last time I ran across this gang of preteens, they knocked the tablet out of my hands. Nothing could happen to the tablet. All of the wedding files were on there.

The little girl and I looked at each other. She was probably five and supercute, with brown hair and big dark eyes. She wore a pretty lavender dress decorated with tiny silk flowers. If Mom had put me into that dress when I was her age, it would be covered with mud and engine grease in about five minutes. When I was five, I either played outside or in Grandma Frida's garage, while she repaired tanks and field artillery.

"Hi," I said. "I'm Catalina."

"Mia Rosa García Ramírez Arroyo del Monte."

I had seen her before, I realized. She always seemed to follow Mrs. Rogan around. She trailed her to the porch, to the study, to the media room. She even wanted to sit next to her in the dining room.

Mia Rosa thrust her unicorn up. It was almost as big as she was and decorated with blue and silver plastic jewels the size of grapes and way too many sparkles.

"This is Sapphire."

"She is very pretty."

"She lives in the midnight clouds and her horn glows with moonlight."

Of course. *Jewel Legends*. It was a popular kid cartoon with mythical animals. I was too old for it, but

Arabella, my younger sister, caught the very beginning of it. Everything had to be *Jewel Legends* for a while: notebooks, backpacks, phone cases . . . And then she went to high school and that was the end of that.

"I want a sparkly gun," Mia Rosa announced in a slightly accented voice.

"Um, what?"

"There is a gun that lets you put more sparklies."

"You want a bedazzler?"

Mia Rosa nodded several times. "Yes. My mommy said you were the go girl and I should ask you."

Go girl. I hid a sigh. "I'll see what I can do. What is your mommy's name, so I know where to deliver the bedazzler?"

"Teresa Rosa Arroyo Roberto del Monte. Thank you. But don't give it to mommy. Give it to me."

Awww. She said thank you. "You're welcome."

She curtsied and ran after the kids, dragging her unicorn.

My phone chimed. I glanced at the text message. Arabella has written, "Where are you??? Get here!!!" and added a gif of a crying baby with photoshopped rivers of tears. I took off at a near run.

It all started with Nevada firing the wedding planner. The first wedding planner.

Usually my older sister was a perfectly reasonable person. Well, as reasonable as someone can be when she is a human lie detector. However, two weeks ago Simon Nightingale disappeared, and House Nightingale hired us to find him. Just three months ago our family registered as a House, and our small PI firm went from Baylor Investigative Agency to House Baylor Investigative Agency. The Nightingale case was our first investigation. The entire Houston elite was watching us, and it drove Nevada a little nuts. A lot nuts. She was pretty much a nutcase.

The first wedding planner was fired because she argued with Nevada. My sister would explain the way she wanted things done and the planner would tell why they couldn't do it that way. Most of the time "couldn't" meant "we won't do it because it's a Prime wedding and it's not the way things are done." Finally, the planner explained to Nevada that it wasn't really her wedding, but a wedding of House Rogan and she needed to stop impeding it with "ridiculous demands," such as serving *queso* as an appetizer at the rehearsal dinner. The planner was promptly escorted from the premises.

The second planner was fired, because she kept lying. Her approach to wedding planning was to pacify the bride by pretending that everything was under control even when it wasn't. She didn't want to be micromanaged. But, my sister was an epic control freak and her attention to detail was legendary within the family. Nevada would ask if something was a problem, and the planner would repeatedly assure her that things were fine, despite being warned that Nevada could sense her lies. Things came to a head when Nevada asked her point-blank if she and Mrs. Rogan had come to an agreement on the caterer. After being told for the tenth time to not worry about it, Nevada snapped. I realized that the second planner was let go when I saw her running to her car in five-inch heels with a look of pure panic on her face. My sister had burst onto the porch behind her, yelling, "Is it fine now? Is it still fine?"

We didn't bother with a third wedding planner. Arabella and I took a weekend, armed ourselves with takeout, and after thirty odd episodes of *Whose Wedding Is It Anyway?* and four seasons of *Bridezilla*, we decided to plan the wedding ourselves. It was that or there would be no wedding.

Unfortunately, while Rogan and his mother treated us with perfect courtesy, the rest of his family wasn't quite sure about our status. Both Arabella and I were registered as Primes, but our records were sealed. Also, our family wasn't wealthy, and Rogan was a billionaire. With me being eighteen and Arabella turning sixteen, they didn't feel we had any authority. I had a feeling we ranked as "poor relatives who run errands," somewhere just above hired help. Apparently, I was the go girl. I didn't even want to know what Arabella was.

Just what I needed. I already felt like a clumsy trespasser in all of this beautiful luxury. This wasn't my home. My home was in the loft of the warehouse. If there was any way to not be here, I would've taken it. But I loved my sister.

It would be a lot easier if we could do all this in Rogan's house, but Rogan and Nevada declared Rogan's home a wedding-free zone and hid there whenever they could.

I turned the corner and walked into a room where Nevada stood on a dais, wearing high-heeled shoes and the in-progress wedding dress, which currently was muslin marked with blue pencil lines. Two people crawled around her, pinning the hem.

Arabella stood in front of her, her arms crossed over her chest. Both Nevada and Arabella were blond, but Nevada's hair was closer to clover honey, while Arabella's resembled gold corn silk. I was the only brunette in the family, besides Mom. Right now the similarities between my two sisters were really apparent, and if you didn't look at their faces, Arabella seemed like a shorter smaller copy of Nevada.

Ooo, I should tell her that next time we fought. She would hate that.

"What is it?" I asked.

"She wants lilacs in her wedding bouquet."

"Okay . . ." Nevada had said she wanted carnations, but we could stuff some pretty pink lilacs in there. I didn't see the problem.

"Blue," Arabella squeezed out. "She wants blue lilacs."

No and also no. "Nevada . . ."

"I had to hide in a bush of French lilacs yesterday and they were very pretty and smelled nice. The card on the tree said, 'Wonder Blue: prolific in bloom and lush in perfume.'"

I googled French lilac, Wonder Blue. It was blue. Like in your face blue. "Why were you hiding in a bush?"

"She was being shot at," Arabella said with a sour face.

"So you stopped to smell the lilacs while people were shooting at you?" I couldn't even.

"Mmm. I was in a greenhouse and they made a lovely hiding spot."

I decided to go with logic. My sister was a logical person. "You asked for a spring wedding. You chose pink, white, and very light sage green as your colors. There is no blue anywhere in the wedding."

"Now there is."

"Your bouquet has pink carnations, pink sweet pea flowers, white roses, and baby breath." *Three* varieties of pink carnations, because she couldn't pick one. And Nevada would never know the panic in the floral designer's eyes when we told her it had to be a carnation bouquet. Apparently, carnations weren't upscale enough for Mad Rogan's wedding. Poor woman kept trying to suggest orchids.

"And blue lilacs," Nevada said.

"It will clash," Arabella growled.

I googled sage bridesmaid dress, held the tablet toward Nevada, and scrolled through images. "Look at the flowers. Pink and white. Pink. Pink. White. Pink and white."

"I don't care," Nevada said. "I want blue lilacs."

And I want to fly away from here, but that wouldn't happen anytime soon, would it?

"Anyway, I have to get back to the office," Nevada said. "Text me if anything."

"The queen has dismissed us," Arabella announced.

I dropped into a deep curtsy. "Your Majesty."

"I hate you guys."

"We hate you back," Arabella told her.

"We hated you before the wedding."

"Before it was cool to hate you."

"Get out!" Nevada growled.

I walked out of the room.

Arabella caught up with me. "We can't do lilacs. It ruins the theme."

"I know."

"What are we going to do?"

"Sleep on it," I told her. "Let's go home."

"Catalina," a woman called.

I turned toward the sound. Arrosa Rogan, Nevada's future mother-in-law waved at me from the doorway, from her wheelchair.

"May I speak to you in private, dear?"

Oh-oh. This couldn't be good. "Yes, ma'am."

"I'll wait for you outside," Arabella said.

Chapter 2

I FOLLOWED MRS. ROGAN deeper into the room. The large office spread before me, walls and walls of bookshelves filled with books of every age, thickness, and color. Daylight spilled from the large arched windows on the right, and the polished floor of cream marble gleamed where sun rays touched it. Each window came with a reading bench equipped with turquoise cushions and ornate pillows. Mexican blankets, white, black, and lavender, were folded on each bench. Delicate Moroccan lanterns hung from the ornate ceiling that was painted with an intricate geometric pattern of pink, white, and blue.

It should've clashed, but instead it all melded into a perfect blend of Texas, Spain, and Morocco. There was something magical about it. Like opening a book of fairy tales and stepping through the pages into some fantasy castle. And Mrs. Rogan glided through it all with effortless elegance, a graceful queen of the palace. Even her wheelchair somehow fit.

I looked down on the floor. Of course, she fit here. She belonged here. It was her house. It wasn't anyone's fault that this house made me feel weird. Being here was like walking through an expensive furniture store or a museum filled with priceless antiques and being afraid to touch anything. It was someone else's space and I just wanted to get out of it and go back to the familiar space of our warehouse.

"I would like to show you something." A heavy leather-bound volume slid from the top shelf and floated to Mrs. Rogan's hand. She opened it.

I came closer and stood on her left. On a thick page an old, yellowed photograph showed a man in a dark uniform and a beautiful woman in a black dress with a black veil, holding a bouquet of white flowers in her hand. A beautiful tiara secured the veil. In its center, under the highest peak, sat a stunning jewel shaped like a heart. It had to be the size of a walnut and it glittered even through the old worn paper.

"My great-grandmother at her wedding," Mrs. Rogan said.

"Oh wow. But the dress is black."

"Traditional Spanish wedding dresses are black." Mrs. Rogan smiled. "Catholicism has this slightly morbid part to it. By wearing a black dress, Catholic women promise to love their husband until death."

That was a little morbid. Who wants to think about death during a wedding?

"Black dresses for devotion and orange blossoms for fertility and happiness. The white wedding dresses didn't come into fashion until British royals adopted it in the 19th century. Elite European families followed suit, but my great-grandmother was a holdout."

Mrs. Rogan turned the page. Another beautiful bride, in a white dress this time, next to a groom in a black suit. The gown's silk train was fanned out in front of them across the floor. The same tiara secured a beautiful veil.

"My grandmother."

"She is very beautiful."

"Thank you."

Another turn of the page. A third bride in a white dress cinching her waist next to a man in a tuxedo, with a 1960's hairstyle. The same crown holding back a veil that blew in the wind, but this time the photograph was in color and the blue green of the jewel took my breath away.

"My mother," Mrs. Rogan said.

"She is also very beautiful."

Why don't we have this? As soon as I got home, I would buy a photo album online and get Grandma Frida and Mom to cough up their wedding pictures.

"Thank you."

Mrs. Rogan turned the page and I saw her, young and radiant, next to a man who looked like Mad Rogan.

She was glowing. Her gown was delicate like spider-webs. The tiara perched on her dark hair as if it always belonged there.

"Wow."

Mrs. Rogan laughed. "Thank you so much for cheering me up. I'm going to add Nevada's picture to this album. Rogan is my only child, but I will be gaining a daughter and her picture will belong in this album."

"She will be very honored," I told her.

"Did you notice the tiara?" she asked.

"Yes. It's gorgeous."

"It's called the Sealight Crown. Technically it's a kokoshnik, not a crown, but crown sounds more impressive. The jewel is an aquamarine. Most people don't know this, but natural aquamarine is often found in sea foam color. They heat it to achieve the light blue. But this stone hasn't been altered in any way. This particular shade of blue green is important to our family."

Rogan had given Nevada a beautiful necklace with a pendant. She thought it was an emerald at the time, but it turned out to be Tear of the Aegean, a one-of-a-kind blue-green diamond. Now it totally made sense.

"Will you let Nevada wear the tiara?" I probably shouldn't have asked that. It was rude.

"I was counting on it. After the wedding, the Sealight will belong to her and she can pass it on to her and Connor's children." Mrs. Rogan sighed. "One small problem."

"Yes?"

"The crown is missing."

"WHAT DO YOU mean it's missing?"

Concern flickered over Mrs. Rogan's features. "It was in its usual place two days ago and it's not there today. Unfortunately, we have to conclude that it was stolen."

Considering how many people had been in and out of the house, it wasn't shocking. We vetted everyone, but background checks never told you the whole picture. A landscaping crew prepared the grounds for the wedding, carpenters were building the custom arbor, another crew was raising an enormous clear tent, at least eight people were hanging lights on the trees, the interior designer and her people, the furniture delivery people . . . That would be a lot of people to interview. It would take Nevada at least two hours. Getting her to sit still for that long would be a challenge.

"The Sealight is tagged with a sensor," Mrs. Rogan said. "It's embedded into the crown and cannot be removed without destroying the tiara. The system can track it through a satellite with the accuracy of up to one mile. Right now, it's telling me that the tiara is still on the premises. I would like you to find it."

Me? I had worked for our agency since I was twelve, first doing small things like surveillance and answering phones, then moving on to my own jobs, but none of my cases were that significant. Mostly, I dealt with insurance fraud because it was low risk, and runaway teens because kids told me things they wouldn't usually tell an adult. This was a big leap.

"We would . . ." I was a rude idiot. I should thank her for her confidence. "I mean, thank you for trusting me. But we must sort through at least a hundred employees, many of them new to the estate. Nevada can do it in a fraction of the time it would take me, and she would do so with complete accuracy. My sister never had a false positive."

"I don't think the culprit is an employee." Mrs. Rogan looked like she'd bitten into a lime. "I'm confident it's a member of my family."

"Why?"

Mrs. Rogan turned to the bookcase. A section of it— six feet wide and twelve shelves high, all crammed to the brim—rose about one-eighth of an inch off the floor and moved toward us.

I held my breath. The weight had to be enormous.

The bookshelves slid past us and gently landed on the floor, revealing a short passage leading to a round chamber. The lights came on, highlighting persimmon-colored walls pitted with alcoves and niches, each holding a treasure: statues, jeweled daggers, scrolls and books in vacuum-sealed cases, and in the center, in the place of prominence, a niche with a bare jewelry holder.

I remembered to breathe.

"Moving the bookcase by normal means would take several people," Mrs. Rogan said. "They would have to unload the books, slide it out without damaging the floor, then slide it back in and fill it with books. I was in this office for the entire afternoon yesterday and almost the entire day the day before that. At night the office is locked and secured by several alarms installed by Connor's people. To disarm them, the perpetrator would have needed the code and my thumbprint. The windows here face the cliff, and they are secured by alarms as well."

Although most biometric security systems were difficult to bypass, it could be done. Fingerprints and even irises could be digitally cloned by using pictures, sometimes the ones taken with a regular cell phone. "Who knows the code?"

"Connor and I. The house server logs every time the door opens, and there were no log-in attempts after I locked the office for the night."

"Do you lock the office during the day if you leave it for a short period of time?"

"No. Children like to play here, and since only a powerful telekinetic can open the vault, I didn't think anyone would touch it."

I glanced at the corners where the security camera watched over us. "What about the security feed?"

Mrs. Rogan looked sheepish. "The cameras aren't on."

"Why?"

She sighed. "Because a woman has a right to privacy inside her own house. The cameras that cover ingress and egress points are always on and the security footage is monitored by Connor's people, but I don't want strangers watching me inside my home. We compromised."

Knowing my future brother-in-law, he wouldn't have liked that one bit. Connor Rogan was deeply paranoid when it came to security. Nevada was too. I shuddered to think what their kids would be like.

"You see now," Mrs. Rogan said. "There was no opportunity to remove the Sealight by ordinary means. The culprit is a powerful telekinetic, which makes this a family affair. And that's exactly why I don't want to involve your sister. I've had an opportunity to observe Nevada over the past three months and I have both respect and affection for your sister."

"Then why not let her handle this?"

Mrs. Rogan folded her hands on her lap. "My son doesn't care for some family members on my side. He has perfectly justifiable reasons for it. They are difficult, entitled, and often ungrateful. However, they are still my relatives. I remember playing in the garden with my brothers and sisters, the trips to the beach, and the family celebrations. I have hopes that we will mend the gulf widening between us. If we ask your sister to handle this theft, she will interrogate the family."

Made sense to me. "And you don't want that?"

"No. Nevada's first introduction to the family can't be that of interrogation and suspicion."

Not to mention that when my sister really used her magic, she could paralyze her target and pry all of their secrets out of their minds. Those who experienced it never forgot it. That's why our paternal grandmother, Victoria Tremaine, was so feared by other Primes.

"I know that you have a lot on your plate already," Mrs. Rogan said. "I'm sorry, but I don't have anyone else to ask. If I go to Connor, my son will hold his relatives upside down one by one and shake them until they confess."

Which would be a lot of fun to watch.

"You have investigative experience and I want to keep this within our family. Will you do this for me? As a favor."

"Of course," I said. "And it's not a favor. Family members don't owe favors to each other."

Those assholes stole my sister's crown. Nevada would wear the Sealight to her wedding even if I had to tear the house down to the slab to find it.

I faced Mrs. Rogan. "I understand that your condition is that Nevada can't know?"

"Yes."

"I have some conditions too. First, I will need access and authority to question your relatives. I can't get very far if they refuse to answer me."

"Not a problem," she said.

"I will need access to your security footage. I would also like to place some additional surveillance cameras inside. They will be monitored by my cousin, not an outsider, and we will remove them once the tiara is found."

"Can this be avoided?"

"No." One of the first things I learned about investigation is to gather as much information as I could.

"Very well." Mrs. Rogan nodded.

"Lastly, I have to tell Connor."

"As long as he doesn't interfere."

"I also have to warn you," I said. I've heard Nevada give this speech before and it felt odd to repeat it. "When an investigation includes members of one's family, we often find something that everyone wishes would've stayed buried. You have to be prepared for that possibility."

Mrs. Rogan considered it. "If one of them jeopardized my son's wedding, I want them found. And punished. The family will forgive the embarrassment, but not the betrayal."

Chapter 3

I CLIMBED INTO the blue Honda Element we borrowed from Mom. Our car options were limited. Most of the cars we owned were older and nondescript, so they wouldn't be noticed during surveillance, and the Element was the best-looking available vehicle we had.

"What's going on?" Arabella asked.

"Mrs. Rogan wants my help with a theft."

Arabella's eyes lit up. "What got stolen?"

"A wedding tiara."

"Does Nevada know?"

"No. And we are going to keep it that way. We have to stop by Rogan's."

"What am I, a chauffeur?"

"I drove here, you drive back."

The trip between our house and Mrs. Rogan's mansion ran about three or three and a half hours, depending on traffic. Normally, we could do a lot of things remotely, but as the wedding drew closer, we ended up making the drive more and more often. And because we were a new House and our sister was marrying Mad Rogan, both of them insisted that we never take the trip alone.

Arabella wrinkled her nose. "Yes, but Rogan's is half an hour out of the way."

I pulled out twenty bucks. "Fine, you've been formally retained." I would expense the agency for it.

Arabella snatched the money out of my hands. "Mine."

"Let's go."

My sister's eyes narrowed. "In a minute."

I looked in the direction of her stare. A young guy was walking toward us. He was lean, with a dark wavy haircut long on top. He had a handsome face with chocolate-brown eyes, wide eyebrows, and full lips. His jaw was clean shaven. He had to be at least my age, but there was something slightly teen idol about him, something deliberately messy but at the same time polished, as if he got out of bed, tousled his hair, accidentally rolled into designer clothes, and now he was just wandering around, not sure what to do with himself and being slightly apologetic for being so handsome.

"He is walking this way," Arabella said.

"If you drive off now, we won't have to talk to him."

"I want to talk to him. He's cute."

Ugh. "Drive."

"No. You're like an old lady sometimes."

Ugh.

The guy reached us. For a moment I thought he would go on Arabella's side, but he changed his course and knocked on my window. Oh great. Just great. I wished I could melt into the car seat.

My window slid down. I would kill my sister.

He leaned on the roof of our car, so he could look into the window, and smiled. He had such a nice smile. It lit his face.

No. No, you can't like his smile. You know what happens when you like people. Stop it.

"Hi," he said.

"Hi," Arabella said.

He was looking at me. "Hello," I said.

"I keep seeing you around," he told me. "And keep trying to say hi. You're always so busy."

You said it, now go.

"I'm Xavier," he said.

I waited for Arabella to jump in, but for once in her life she suddenly decided to keep her mouth shut. Traitor.

"I'm Catalina," I said.

He smiled again. "I know."

This was a stupid conversation.

"Do you like tennis?" he asked.

Who what? Say something . . .

"She loves it," Arabella piped up.

"Maybe we could play sometime." He shrugged.

"Sorry, I know it's lame, but the nearest town is an hour away and they won't let me drive. There isn't much to do here. So, what do you say?"

"Sure." This was the quickest way to get rid of him.

"Great. See you around."

He stepped away, gave me another dazzling smile, and walked away. I raised my window. Arabella drove out of the courtyard.

"*She loves it?* I don't even know how to play!"

"He doesn't care about tennis. He knows your name."

"I know that," I growled. "You know I can't."

"No, you won't. You've been controlling your magic much better."

"I can't take the risk."

"No, you won't even try." Arabella shook her head.

"It's irresponsible!"

"Hanging out with a cute guy is irresponsible. Listen to yourself. You're eighteen, not thirty."

"I can't treat people like toys. I might start liking him. I might want to hang out with him."

"And?"

"And sometimes that's how little it takes."

"Why don't you give up and be a nun, then!"

"Maybe I will!"

We rode in silence.

"I'm not saying you should fall in love or make out with him or chase him around screaming, 'wife me now!'" Arabella said.

"I know."

"All I'm saying is that you could give him a chance. A tiny chance. A sliver of a chance. What's the worst that can happen?"

"My control might slip a hair. My magic might leak. He'll become besotted because of my magic and follow me around with a slack look on his face listening to my every word and doing creepy things like stealing hair from my brush so he can hide it under his pillow and sniff it at night when he gets lonely."

Arabella looked at me. "That was oddly specific."

"Michael Sanchez in my freshman year. Eyes on the road."

"Suppose this happens." My sister merged into the middle lane. "Let's say he becomes 'besotted.' So what? He is leaving in a week. Your magic wears off with time and distance. Even if the worst happens, in a month he will be fine. People take that long to get over normal summer flings."

"It still isn't right." I had no right to manipulate other people's feelings. It didn't matter that I wouldn't have meant to do it. The possibility existed.

"Do you remember the ranch?"

The ranch was owned by one of Mom's friends, two hundred acres of scrub and rocks in the middle of nowhere. We would take Arabella there, so she could metamorphose without anyone freaking out.

"We went to the ranch, so I could practice. And I went every time and I did my best. Even when I was twelve and a crazy ball of rage, because I knew that if I wanted to have any kind of life, I had to learn my magic. I had to figure out what I could do, how long I could do it, what I couldn't do. It's like driving and learning where the car ends and how quickly it can stop. You don't practice."

I glared at her. "I practice all the time."

"Yes, you practice not using it. You're excellent at not using your power. You've got that part down."

"I *am* excellent at not using it. I have to be."

Arabella's eyes narrowed. "Then Xavier is in no danger, is he?"

She got me. "I hate you sometimes."

"You hate that I'm right. Seriously, what's the harm in talking to Xavier? You're going to college in the fall. There's going to be all kinds of people there. Guys, Catalina. There will be cute *college* guys."

"Maybe I won't go to college."

"Sure," Arabella said.

I didn't say anything.

"Wait, are you serious?"

"Yes."

"Why?"

Why was complicated. There were many reasons. It was expensive. I didn't know what I wanted to major in and I didn't want to waste my time and the family's money. But most of all, I had spent the last four years racing to the graduation finish line trying to get the highest score in everything. I had existed in a state of constant pressure, where something was always due and once I finished it, I was already behind on the next paper, the next exam, or the next project. When they finally ran out of courses to give me and I finished this Christmas, I felt like I had breathed fresh air for the first time since I started high school. They were still making me come back for the graduation and walk across the stage. I would graduate this May. I would finally be free.

And when I told Mom and Grandma Frida that, there would be hell to pay. I had scored 1580 on the SAT out of a possible 1600. I was in the top 1 percent nationwide. I had my pick of schools. I could get a scholarship almost anywhere. They would tell me I was throwing away my future.

"Even if you don't go to college, you have to interact with people outside the family eventually. I don't want you to be alone, Catalina. If you want to be alone, that's fine, but I don't want you to be forced to be alone because you think you have no choice. If it was just about magic, then you could've gone out with Alessandro. He is an Antistasi Prime. He could've resisted you."

She had to bring that up. "He had been exposed to the full power of my magic."

Arabella grimaced. "Oh don't give me that. I've seen people after you charmed them. He had none of the symptoms. All he wanted to do was take you for a drive in his fancy car and to talk to you. You threatened to call the cops on him. Seriously, what are you afraid of?"

"That it wouldn't be real." The words dropped like

bricks. "Nobody ever likes me for me, Arabella." And I had really wanted him to.

Silence stretched.

Arabella reached out and petted my hand. She kept petting it, like I was a dog.

"Quit it."

"There there."

"I said quit touching me."

"How can they ever like you for you if you never talk to them? Who outside of the family knows you? It's a serious question. Are people supposed to telepathically scan you to make friends?"

I groaned. "If I give Xavier a chance, will you shut up?"

"Yes!"

"Then fine. If he comes up to me again, I will talk to him. Happy?"

"Ecstatic."

"Good."

She had a point. I couldn't keep complaining that nobody liked me for me if I didn't give anyone the opportunity to see who I was. Maybe if I started small. Just one boy. Just one conversation. I would keep a steel hold on my magic.

Maybe it wouldn't be so bad.

I LIKED ROGAN's house much better than his mother's mansion. It was still filled with expensive furniture, but it felt different—simpler, rugged. More like a home and less like a palace. Being here was almost like being in the warehouse. I had called ahead to make sure Rogan would be there, but we could've just showed up and nobody would have been surprised.

I rang the doorbell. The door swung open, revealing a sturdy man with broad shoulders and short blond hair. Like most of Rogan's people, he was ex-military.

"Ladies," Troy said. "I'm authorized to tell you there is sushi in the kitchen."

"Ooo." My sister veered off and made a beeline for the kitchen.

"The Major is waiting for you in the office," Troy said.

"Thanks." I climbed the stairs, crossed the balcony, and entered the business part of the house, where Rogan conducted his affairs. I waved at people I knew on the way until I got to the surveillance room, where a thin wiry man with dark hair sat in front of nine monitors. He spun his chair around when he heard me coming. His face twitched.

"Hi Bug."

"Hi."

Bug was a swarmer. Swarms existed in the arcane realm. Nobody knew much about the arcane realm or the creatures within it. Summoners and other arcane mages could reach into it and draw things out, but they didn't really understand it.

For example, it was an established fact that implanting a swarm in a human would skyrocket their surveillance capabilities, allowing them to process visual information at an insane rate. It was also an established fact that these augmented humans died within a couple of years. Bug had volunteered for the procedure during his time in the Air Force. Everything went as planned. He survived the implantation process, became a swarmer, and received a substantial bonus. There was just one snag—Bug didn't die. When Nevada first found him, he was borderline insane. Somehow Rogan managed to fix him and now Bug presided over all of Rogan's surveillance.

"Xavier Ramírez Secada," he said. "Age 19, first son and heir of Iker Ramírez Madrid and Eva Secada Escudero. Rated as a bottom tier Significant Telekinetic. He likes to tell people that he is Rogan's *Sobrino*."

"So?"

"He is not Rogan's nephew. His father, Iker Ramírez, is Rogan's cousin, which makes Xavier *Primo Segundo* or first cousin once removed. Hard pass, Catalina. *Hard* pass."

"Stay out of my life, Bug." I kept walking.

"His Instagram is called Boss Moves," he yelled.

"Stay out!"

I took another turn and came to Rogan's office. Most of the time he used the room adjacent to Bug's nest, but once in a while he hid in the back, in his study. I knocked on the heavy red oak door. It swung open, inviting me inside.

Like his mother, Rogan devoted the entire wall, floor

to ceiling, to books, but here the wood was dark, the chairs were soft chocolate leather, and the floor was old weathered wood. Rogan sat behind a large desk, his fingers dancing over the keyboard of a laptop. A chair slid out for me. I sat. A large glass with an extra wide straw floated over and waited in empty air, motionless. I took it and sipped. Mmm, lychee boba tea. My favorite.

I didn't know if Rogan genuinely liked us, or if he treated us well because we were important to Nevada and he loved her. I liked to think he liked us.

Rogan looked up from his laptop. "Budget update?"

"In your in-box."

He checked the file. "A bedazzler for $19.99?"

"It's a small gun that attaches rhinestones to fabric."

He frowned. "Is that for her veil? Because you know I can't have anything to do with that."

My sister and Rogan had reached a compromise. Neither of them had wanted an expensive wedding. Our family couldn't go half and half with Rogan either, not on the scale this wedding was happening, so it was decided that since Mrs. Rogan wouldn't be denied, we would buy the dress, veil, shoes, and the bouquet, and Rogan would pay for everything else. Rogan would've been happy to pay for all of it, but Nevada insisted, and if she found out we went around her in any way, there would be hell to pay.

"No, the bedazzler isn't for the veil. It's for Mia Rosa García Ramírez Arroyo del Monte's stuffed unicorn."

"Okay then. Next?"

"Sealight is missing," I told him.

There was a second of silence.

"Those assholes stole it," he said.

Wow. He went right to it.

"Mrs. Rogan asked me to look into it. She wants it handled quietly, and she doesn't want Nevada involved."

Rogan sighed. "Of course. The less my future wife has to do with those dickheads the better."

"Are all of them dickheads?"

"No. Uncle Inigo, his wife Emilia, and their three kids have my complete confidence. Same for Uncle Mattin and his family. I don't agree with his politics, but he would never dishonor the family name. We can scratch them off the list. Aunt Miren and her daughter, Cousin Gracia, are women of impeccable integrity, and I trust Gracia's wife and their two children. But the younger of my mother's siblings are perfectly capable of stealing from the bride at the wedding."

I leaned back. "Tell me about it?"

He sighed. "My grandfather is one of those men who believes that children belong to their mothers until they are old enough to contribute to the family business. He is an old cantankerous bastard. He married my grandmother and had four children, including my mother. When mom was ten years old, her mother died, leaving my grandfather with four kids and no idea how to raise them. As soon as he was done with mourning, he remarried. The second wife was only twelve years older than my mother. He married her because she had the right pedigree, the right set of powers, and was young and healthy. I've met her. She was very young when she married, and she had dreams of a loving husband and a beautiful family, and instead she found herself relegated to the role of a glorified babysitter, whom my grandfather mostly ignored."

That wasn't fair.

"My grandfather had three children with her. By the time the last one was born, the older children were grown and assumed their responsibilities, so they received the lion's portion of his attention. The three younger ones were left to fend for themselves and their mother denied them nothing. They grew up hedonistic and entitled. They have a deep disdain for our side of the family and once the old man dies, the family will likely split. But my mother remembers them as the cute babies whom she looked after. She is determined to forgive them their faults, and they are perfectly willing to use her. The only time I hear from them is when they want something: money, influence, guarantees, and so on. Aside from that they don't even bother with basic maintenance like sending her Christmas cards. So you have Inigo, Mattin, Miren, and my mother on one side and Markel, Ane, and Zorion on the other."

I checked my tablet for the houseguest chart, which I grabbed from Mrs. Rogan's desktop before leaving. They had put the three oldest siblings and their children in the east wing and the three half siblings and their children in the west. That made my job easier. "Your grandfather isn't coming to the wedding?"

"No. He had an odd rivalry with my father. It was one-sided, but now that Dad is gone, he's carried it over to me. His health is failing, and he doesn't want anyone, especially me, to know it."

"Could any of your relatives open Mrs. Rogan's vault?"

Rogan grimaced. "It's possible. They pride themselves on hiding the full extent of their powers. It's a family sport. Curiously, it keeps the peace. Nobody is sure how strong everyone is, so nobody wants to risk a confrontation. Most of that side of the family ranks in the Significant range, but once in a while, usually once per generation, they produce an off-the-charts Prime. My mother is one. My father came to Basque country because she matched the right set of powers he wanted in a bride and once he met her, he refused to let her go. He'd signed off almost half of his capital over to her father to marry her."

"So, your grandfather sold her?"

"Pretty much. Ask her to tell you the story sometime."

Better and better. "Who would know that cameras in the office are nonfunctioning?"

"Everyone. Mother assured everyone that they would have privacy inside the house."

We stared at each other with identical expressions.

Sometimes Mom did things like this. Like when we said, "don't climb into the crow's nest today, because your leg is hurting," and she would do it anyway and then spend the evening rubbing Icy Hot into her knee and limping.

"I'm going to bug the house," I told him.

"Did my mother agree to this?"

"Yes, on the condition that nobody except family views the recording. Bern is family."

Rogan leaned back. "You got further than I have in the last twelve years. Congratulations."

"Thank you. She really wants the Sealight found. She showed me the wedding album."

"What do you need from me?"

"I need files on everyone, even people you don't suspect. I need someone to sneak in as part of the landscaping crew and install the cameras. I could get Bern to do it, but if they had done their homework, they will recognize him, and I don't want to take chances. Also, I would like you to take over the monitoring of the Sealight sensor."

"Which is an antique." Rogan grimaced again.

"I want to be notified immediately if the tiara leaves the grounds."

"Very well," he said.

"Also, I need you to convince Nevada that blue lilacs don't belong in her bouquet."

His eyes flashed. "Nice try. You're on your own."

"It was worth a shot."

Chapter 4

PEOPLE SAID THAT the kitchen was the heart of the house. If that was true, what would it make the kitchen table? One of the atriums, because food flowed into it, or one of the ventricles, because we ate the food and flowed out? Sometimes weird things like that got stuck in my brain. Usually when I was tired, and my brain wanted to do something else.

I rubbed my face and drank more coffee. The table was covered with tablets and notepads. On my right, my cousin Bern was messing with hummingbirds— tiny waterproof cameras in casings that could be tinted the color of your choice. We decided to hide them in the pretty shrubs. Bern was a huge blond bear of a guy, the cameras were tiny, and he handled them with the precision of a surgeon. He was the oldest of all of us, except for Nevada.

Across the table Arabella was going over the catering menu on her tablet. When Mrs. Rogan was a child, she was almost poisoned at a birthday party. Her little cousin had died instead. Now she prepared most of her food herself, but that wasn't an option for the wedding. Nevada deferred to Mrs. Rogan, and after interviewing seventeen catering companies, she finally settled on one. Now we had to select the menu, and Mrs. Rogan had delayed till the last minute.

Next to Arabella, Bern's brother, Leon, dark and lean, had taken apart some sort of a gun and was cleaning it. Ever since Leon discovered his magic talent a few months ago it was all guns all the time. Mom didn't even try to stop him anymore. She was by the sink, trying to precision pour melted gelatin into silicone molds. Arabella had told her that there was no way homemade gummy bears would ever taste the same as store-bought. Now half the fridge was occupied with silicone trays.

My brain hummed, trying to sort through the background files on the two branches of the family Rogan suspected.

We all used to sit just like this when we did our homework.

"What's a canapé?" Arabella asked.

"Something with a melon on it," Leon said.

"It's a bread thing," Bern said.

A door swung open deep in the warehouse and a couple of moments later Grandma Frida emerged wearing a pair of heavy-duty twill overalls, smudged with engine grease. Her platinum white curls framed her face like a halo and her blue eyes sparkled. Grandma Frida was almost never in a bad mood. I once asked her why and she said she didn't have that much time left so she didn't want to waste it being miserable. I obsessed over every cough she made for a month after that.

"Grandma, what's a canapé?" Arabella asked.

Grandma Frida landed in her chair and wrinkled her nose. "Isn't it an Italian desert with cream in it?"

"That's cannoli," Mom said.

"Just google it," Leon said.

Arabella growled under her breath. "Every time I shrink their order window, it resets, and my phone is dead."

I passed her mine.

"How is it going?" Mom asked.

"If I eliminate everyone under the age of ten and everyone Rogan has vouched for, it leaves me with 12 primary suspects," I said.

"An adult could get a kid to do their dirty deed," Grandma Frida said.

"Yes, but anyone under the age of ten would tell," I said.

"These kids run around the house in packs, unsupervised," Arabella said. "They would blab. Also, Bern was right. Canapé is a bread thing."

I studied my list of suspects. I had them organized room by room in the west wing, going north to south. The Spanish names were terribly confusing and some of them were very long, so for the sake of clarity, I culled them down to one given name and one married name. The main last name in the family was Ramírez. Mrs. Rogan had three siblings housed in the west wing, her two half brothers, Markel and Zorion, and her half sister, Ane.

First, there was Markel, Mrs. Rogan's oldest half brother, and his second wife, Isabella. Markel didn't seem to be employed. He lived off the proceeds from the family's investments. A search of Isabella's Facebook revealed a lavish house and nice cars. However, Rogan's files noted that Markel repeatedly complained in private that his stipend wasn't large enough. None of this stipend seemed to have made it to his son and daughter.

The next room held Mikel Ramírez, Markel's son, and his wife Maria. Mikel managed Ramírez Capital, a venture capital firm owned by the family, with focus on telecommunications and internet companies. He was a tall, pale, dark-haired man with a prematurely greying beard and sad eyes. His wife was a thin, overly tan woman with bleached blond hair, who liked designer clothes, usually in white, and chunky gold jewelry. I had seen her twice. Both times she had a wineglass in her hand and both times she asked if I had seen her husband. They had four children, three under the age of twelve.

Next were Lucian and June de Baldivia. June was Markel's daughter, a plump woman with olive skin and a wealth of dark curly hair. Her husband was tall, athletic, and handsome, with dark hair and narrow, startlingly blue eyes. He jogged around the estate every morning. Lucian worked for a computer firm specializing in cyber security, while June was heavily involved in a start-up trying to clean up plastic from the oceans. They had two daughters, who looked exactly like their mom.

Then, there was Zorion and Teresa Rosa del Monte, the parents of bedazzler girl. Zorion, Mrs. Rogan's youngest half brother, was forty years old, trim, athletic, and handsome. He lived off the family proceeds and seemed to have two interests: soccer and cars. Teresa was a housewife with an edgy pixie cut. She took care of their two children and was trying to write a novel. A search of her online activity showed heavy Twitter usage where she stalked a number of romance writers and literary agents, both in and outside of Spain. They weren't in great financial distress.

The next room over was occupied by Ane, Mrs. Rogan's half sister, who had arrived with a boy toy, as Arabella put it. The boy toy was in his late twenties, blond, blue-eyed, pretty, and went by Paul Sarmiento. Ane didn't work, relying on her portion from the family investments as income. Paul didn't have a criminal record and Rogan's people couldn't find his fingerprints in any of the databases, but it wasn't clear what he actually did for a living. I put a check mark by his name.

Finally, in the far south, we had Iker and Eva Ramírez. Iker, Ane's only child, had olive skin and dark blond hair and was an architect. He'd been working at his firm for the last four years. His wife was petite and delicate. She had started her career as an actress, but that went out the window when she married Iker. They had only one child, Xavier.

"One thing I don't understand," Leon said, sliding one gun part into another. He did this without looking down, as if his hands were on autopilot. "Why did they steal the Sealight? They're all rich."

"Let me see a picture of it again," Grandma Frida asked.

I pulled up an image of the Sealight and showed it to her.

Grandma Frida squinted and tapped the aquamarine. "There's your answer."

I shook my head. "I don't think it's about money. The Sealight is appraised and insured for two hundred and fifty thousand, mostly because of its age and the small diamonds framing the aquamarine. The aquamarine heart is worth probably seventy-five thousand by itself. The three black sheep siblings each receive over a million dollars annually from the family's investments. For doing nothing."

"Must be nice," Mom said.

Arabella frowned. "So if they're caught stealing the tiara, they will almost certainly be cut off. Would you risk an easy million to steal something worth a quarter of that?"

Bern clapped his hands. "You did the math in your head, I'm so proud."

Arabella flipped him off.

"I saw that," Mom snapped.

"Sorry." My sister didn't sound sorry.

"Even if they did steal it," I said, "what would they do with it? None of them have been in the US in the past five years. They don't know any fences and no legitimate jeweler would touch it. If you google it, the picture of it comes up as 'The Sealight Crown, heirloom of House Rogan.' Nobody in Texas would touch something stolen from Mad Rogan. They couldn't give it away."

"Maybe they're planning to take it home," Arabella said.

"They would have to declare it at the airport," Leon said.

"How do you know that?" Mom asked.

"He checked into transporting guns by air," Arabella said.

Mom stopped filling the dishwasher and gave Leon a hard stare.

"Just trying to be prepared, that's all," he said.

I leaned back and sighed. "They can't sell it and they can't take it home. So, it's not about the money."

"Well, what is it about then?" Grandma Frida asked.

"It's about Mrs. Rogan, Connor, or Nevada," I said. "Either they hate Mrs. Rogan or Connor, and they want to embarrass them, or they hate Nevada and they don't want her to have it. Which is why she can't know, and we have to handle it and never tell her."

"Agreed," Bern said.

"So, basically, you have to figure out who hates Rogan and Nevada the most," Arabella said. "Is Xavier a suspect?"

Die.

Grandma Frida came to life like a shark smelling a drop of blood in the water. "Who is Xavier?"

"Nobody." What a brilliant response I came up with. That will throw them off the scent. Not.

"Xavier is Rogan's cute cousin, aaannd he likes her," The Evil Hellspawn Sister said.

"If you think he's cute, then you should talk to him," I said.

Arabella made big eyes at me. "She told him her name and he said, 'I know.'"

Grandma Frida and Leon made woo woo noises at me.

My cheeks were getting warm. I hated when my cheeks got warm.

"You should go for it," Grandma Frida said.

That was about enough. "Mom."

"What happened to that handsome Italian boy?" Grandma Frida asked.

"She ran him off," Leon said. "She told him to get off our land or she would call the law." He had growled "the law" like he had a mouth full of gravel.

They were talking about me as if I wasn't even there. "Mom!"

"Let her be," Mom said. "She's trying to do a job."

"Maybe you should give it a try," Grandma Frida said. "You've been doing good with your magic."

"Yeah," Leon said. "And if things don't work out, I can always shoot him, and nobody will ever find the body."

I took my tablet and files and went to my room.

I STOOD NEXT to the ladder in Iker and Eva's room and watched Rivera install a tiny camera into the smoke detector. Rivera was one of Rogan's top guys. Normally he was trim and clean-cut, but today he was wearing a wig under a grimy baseball cap and his jaw sported a dark two-day stubble. He looked ridiculous.

Each of the guest couples had a suite and we were bugging the living rooms. Outside, Simone, one of Rogan's surveillance specialists, was installing hummingbird cameras in the bushes.

"Hey," Xavier said behind me.

I managed to not jump and turned around. He leaned casually against the door frame. Right. It was his room too.

"Hi," I managed.

"Hi," he said.

I'd spent a long time on the drive over to Mountain Rose thinking about what to do if I saw Xavier. I had promised Arabella I would talk to him. Unfortunately, I wasn't very good at talking to people, especially people my age. In the end, I decided I had to talk to Xavier. Not just because he was cute and seemed to want to talk to me, but also because he was a potential lead. He was a teenager and a member of Rogan's extended family. Adults generally viewed us as children, whether they were willing to admit it or not, and they often said things around us without thinking.

Once I decided that Xavier was work, things became a lot easier. I just had to get him to like me without using my magic.

"Do you need something from the room? We're almost done."

"No, I just saw you through the window and wondered what you were doing in my suite. What *are* you doing?"

He sounded like he suspected we had gone through his underwear drawer. Rivera rolled his eyes.

"We're checking all the smoke detectors and replacing the batteries," I lied.

"Why?"

"Mrs. Rogan is worried that if a fire breaks out, some people might not get out."

"Each room in this wing has French doors that open to the garden," Xavier said. "Don't you think it's a bit extra? We're not likely to get trapped and most of us are telekinetics."

He seemed like the poster boy for the "adults are unreasonable and lame" crowd. I went through that phase too. When I was twelve. "True. But, she's paranoid and

I have to do this. You know how it is." I shrugged. "Old people."

Xavier grinned and glanced at Rivera, then back at me. "Do you have to supervise, or can I steal you away for a little bit? I need your help with something."

Rivera's eyes got a dangerous glint. I had to get Xavier out of here before he asked too many questions or said something Rivera would make him regret.

"You got this?" I asked.

"Yes, ma'am," Rivera said.

"Please let me know when you're finished." I turned to Xavier. "Okay."

We walked out into the hallway. Xavier turned left, and we kept going, through a long hallway to the north end of the house, through the French doors and into the other side of the garden. A path of decomposed granite started at the door and veered right, running through the orchard to the northeast side of the hill bordering the cliff.

Xavier started on the path, turned, graceful, and smiled at me. He really was very handsome. Almost as handsome as Alessandro Sagredo, but it was a different kind of beauty. Xavier looked like he would be perfect for the lead role in some angsty show about rich teenagers in a prep school. There was something sophisticated but nonchalant about him. Alessandro looked like he needed a sword and a hat with feathers.

Xavier was cute, but I had really liked Alessandro. I had liked him the first time I saw his picture. I had sat

there for several minutes staring at it, not really thinking about anything at all. It was as if my brain had gone
quiet. That almost never happened. And then I met him,
and I knew there was no way.

"What did you need help with?" I asked.

"I need help with being beyond bored. You're the
only interesting person I've met. Let's do something
fun. You do have that here, don't you?"

"I have to work." *You don't know what you're asking.
If I have fun with you, it won't end well for either of us.*

"What will happen if you stop working for just a little
while?" He shrugged. "Will the house fall down? Will
Arrosa fire you? She can't fire you—you're the bride's
sister. Come on, at least walk with me. Am I really worse
than working?"

No, he wasn't worse than working; he was work. He
was a potential source of information, one I had to ex-
plore. Or was it exploit?

"One second," I said. I opened the chat window on
my tablet and sent Rivera a quick text. Please change
camera placement in Xavier's suite. Rogan's files pegged
Xavier as a low-level Significant, which meant that when
properly motivated, he could likely remove the smoke
detector off the twelve-foot ceiling with his magic and
examine it. I didn't want to take a chance of him finding
the camera.

The tablet pinged back. Got it.

"Okay." I walked down the steps to the path. "I'm
ready. But only until two o'clock."

"What happens at two?" He asked.

"My sister will be presenting the catering menu to Mrs. Rogan and she might need backup." Arabella did not need backup. Most of the time she was the backup, the field artillery, and the air support, but Nevada taught me to always have an exit strategy. I smiled at Xavier, trying to look enthusiastic. "Lead the way."

We strolled down the path.

"Are you worried that guy is going to steal something?"

What? "No, all of the people I hired have been vetted."

"You hired?" He let it hang.

"Yes, well, Arabella and I hired them. We ran an extensive background check, employment history, arrest history, and credit checks. Everyone on the grounds right now has references."

Xavier's nonchalant mask slid off for a second and he stared at me. "How do you know how to do this?"

"It's my job. I work for our family business."

"Yeah, I know. But I thought your family owned the business. I mean, you're a kid like me. Why do they make you work? Are you that . . . poor?" He said the word like it was something dirty or shameful.

I hid a sigh. It wasn't Xavier's fault. He grew up with different standards. It didn't make him better or worse than me, just different. "Nobody makes me work. I like it. Everybody in my family works for the agency. Even my grandmother, who has her own business, sometimes moonlights for us. It's interesting. Sometimes I get to help people. And I never have to ask my mom for money. I get a paycheck, and nobody tells me what to do with it. How does it work for you?"

"We just always have money. If I need something or want something I use my allowance, if I don't have enough, I ask my mom."

"What do you do for your allowance?"

"What?"

"What do you do? Do you get good grades, do chores? Do you help around the house? Mow the lawn?" I winked at him.

"You're teasing me," he said, sounding slightly injured.

"Maybe a little. But seriously, how does it work in your family? I know that Rogan used telekinesis for a lot of military contracts his House has. Are your parents expecting you to use your magic for family business or are they harping about college at you too?"

Xavier shrugged. "I don't think they care. My mother has been making University noises, but it's like she does it because she thinks she has to. My father gets his money from family investments. I don't remember them ever having jobs. Not the kind where they must be there all day. I wish they had jobs. It would get them out of the house."

When I was in middle school, high school scared me to death. I had been homeschooled. So, I researched, and I stumbled onto *How to Win Friends and Influence*

People by Dale Carnegie. I took two things away from that book: people liked to talk about themselves and people liked you when you agreed with them.

"Your parents hover, don't they? I hate when adults do that."

"Yes." He snapped his fingers. "They hover. They don't actually care, they just hang about. They only notice me, so they can drag me to some family bore-fest."

"You didn't want to come to the wedding?" I opened my eyes wide in mock surprise.

"No, I wanted to have the house to myself."

"Yes, I get it. To be honest, I don't feel comfortable here, but then I am a poster girl for monachopsis."

"What?"

"Monachopsis. It means a subtle but nagging feeling of not fitting in and knowing that you don't belong in the place you are. This house is too much. Too big, too many rooms. I didn't grow up wealthy."

"My family has money, but I don't feel comfortable here either." His eyes sparked. His face turned animated, like he was about to ride a roller coaster. "There is wealth. This is Wealth. Capital *w*. Do you know, Rogan is worth $1.27 billion? And there's no prenup. Your sister is going to get half of that. If he dies, she gets all of that."

Well, that got morbid fast.

Xavier smiled. "Good time to suck up, huh?"

I thought of telling him how Nevada was paying for her own wedding dress, but he wouldn't get it.

"You're right. Better be nice."

So far nothing about this conversation made Xavier appealing. He might have been simply uncomfortable talking to me and was trying to say things to impress me, but it was coming out wrong. I had been there.

"Is it true your sister is a Truthseeker Prime?" he asked.

"Yes." Unlike my and Arabella's powers, Nevada's was now public record. Both Arabella and I were registered as Primes, but our records were sealed.

"So, you can't lie to her. Like at all?"

"You can but she'll know." Now was a good time. "Is your family nervous that she's marrying Rogan? Not a lot of families would welcome a Truthseeker."

"She's making them squirm." He grinned. "Your sister walks into the room, and everyone shuts up. Every time Grandma Ane sees her, her face turns green. Cousin Mikel just runs away. I love it."

He hadn't really answered my question.

The path brought us to the front of the house. Two girls my age stood by the fountain, talking. One was tall and blonde, the other was curvier with dark, almost black hair. A third girl, dressed in white, her brown hair braided over her left shoulder, sat on the rim of the fountain typing on her phone. The tall blonde was Gracia's oldest daughter, Adriana; the one with very dark hair was either Samanta or Malina, one of Lucian and June's daughters. They looked so similar, it was hard for me to tell them apart. The girl on the phone was Mikel and Maria's daughter. Like her mother, Elba dressed in white and liked gold jewelry.

Adriana and Samanta—I was 75 percent sure she was Samanta—waved. Adriana noticed me and her eyes narrowed. Samanta looked uncomfortable.

"Don't you know you're not supposed to talk to the help?" Elba asked without looking up from her phone.

Well, hello to you too, Ms. Bitch. I smiled.

"Does your dad know that?" Xavier asked. "How many people has he paid off now—is it three or four? We've all lost count."

"*Que te folle un pez,*" Elba said.

I hope you get fucked by a fish? What did that even mean? Their Spanish was different from what I was used to in Texas, but I understood it well enough.

Xavier put his arm around me and I had to stop myself from driving my elbow into his ribs. I did not like to be touched. Especially by people I didn't know. He did it in a protective way, but I still didn't like it.

"Don't mind her," Xavier said.

We crossed the courtyard back to the west wing. My tablet chimed. I glanced at it. The cameras had come online.

"I have to go."

"Really?" Xavier ducked a little to look at my face. "Are you sure?"

"Yes."

"I had a nice time," he said. He sounded like he meant it. Maybe he did.

The thing was, I kind of had a nice time too. Sure, he said some questionable stuff, but he tried to have an actual conversation with me, and that didn't happen every day. And he tried to protect me from his cousin. I didn't need any help, but it was kind of endearing. Also, he told me that his grandmother and Mikel had something to hide.

"I had a nice time too," I said.

"Then we'll do this again, right?" he asked. "Say yes, Catalina."

He said my name. "Yes. We'll do it again."

I went inside, ducked into one of the conference rooms across from the suites, and checked the feed from the cameras one by one. All of the suite cameras were functioning. I switched to the hummingbird cameras outside. One, two, three, four . . . nine? There should only have been six. I tapped the feed from camera seven. It showed a sitting area on the west side, just outside the building. Camera eight covered the path on the east side from which Xavier and I just came. Camera nine was installed at the top of the fountain. Bern must have wanted additional coverage.

Xavier was walking toward his cousins.

My cell phone rang. I recognized the number. Valentina's House Catering. Oh no. No, no, no. Arabella was in charge of the menu. If they were calling me, there was a problem.

I answered the phone. "Catalina Baylor."

Valentina's voice sounded in my ear. "We've had a tiny, little, itsy-bitsy problem. Someone broke into our restaurant."

Crap. "I'll be right there."

Chapter 5

VALENTINA'S HOUSE CATERING was in New Braunfels, a very German town in the middle of Texas. We had interviewed larger catering firms from Austin and San Antonio, but Mrs. Rogan decided she trusted Valentina's and so that's who we went with.

I parked in front of an old brick building. Leon got out of the passenger seat. Arabella was still in school, and today she was crash-writing a two-thousand-word essay, which was assigned to her a month ago and which she had started this morning. Leon was my battle buddy for this mission and he was thrilled.

"Cake shop," he said.

"Yes."

Leon let out a long-suffering sigh. "Are you sure that I'll be enough? These places can get pretty rough. You walk into a cake shop and then some gunslinger tells you, 'You ain't from around here, partner,' and the next thing you know, you're in the middle of the street, your horse is dead, the bad guy's got your girl by her hair, and you're down to one bullet."

"What is going on in your head?"

"It's a dark, lawless place, Catalina. So dark."

I rolled my eyes. "It's a small restaurant and bakery. Most of their money comes from catering, but they do have a small cupcake shop about two blocks down. Four full-time employees, besides the owner. They hire waitstaff for large events."

"So, we're hiring someone, and they're hiring someone? Who is screening the waitstaff?"

"We are hiring the waitstaff this time," I told him. Rogan had given me a nearly unlimited budget and I made sure to hire waiters with great references. "This is the only place Mrs. Rogan trusts to cater, so we did what we could to secure the location. Rogan's people installed an excellent alarm and security system."

"I thought you said they discovered the break-in this morning." Leon eyed the building.

"Yes, they did."

"So, they didn't arm their excellent alarm system?"

"Let's find out."

Most of the building inside was taken up by a large kitchen. Long metal prep tables stretched across the floor in two rows. On the left two industrial-size refrigerators stood against the wall, along with three large sinks, a dishwasher, and a row of ovens. Next to them a door led to a narrow room with two equally large freezers. Straight ahead, directly opposite the entrance, another door offered access to a large pantry. A row of windows in the wall on our right flooded the space with natural light. It was a clean, uncluttered space. The air smelled faintly of sour wine.

Valentina jumped up from her chair when we entered. A white woman in her midthirties, her short blond hair had a streak of wild purple in it. Her glasses kept sliding down her nose and she kept pushing them back up. Red blotches stained her cheeks. She was clearly stressed out and on the verge of tears. Her XO, Carlos, a solidly built man in his fifties, with black hair and bronze skin, stood next to her, hands on his hips.

"They broke in last night," Valentina said. "Three of them in dark hoodies."

Leon nodded at the first window on our right, with the windowsill stained with grey fingerprint powder. "Is that how they came in?"

"Yes," Carlos said. "We open the windows a lot to air the kitchen out."

"Did the alarm not go off?" I asked.

Both Valentina and Carlos looked like they wanted to fall through the floor.

"The wireless sensor on that window keeps going off randomly," Carlos said.

"Why didn't you notify us that the sensor was malfunctioning?" I asked.

"It didn't seem like a big deal. It's a very small

window. We usually bypass it," Valentina said. "Otherwise it goes off in the middle of the night."

"It's kids." Carlos growled, his face turning dark red. "Probably tried the window, figured out we forgot to lock it, and crawled in. I bet it's that idiot Hudson. Him and his sidekick are always in the park across the street. Up to no good. They sit in the park, drink beer all day, and look for trouble to get into. When I was their age, I had a job. I had responsibilities. I—"

I had to cut him off before it turned into a full-blown lecture about kids these days. "What did they take?"

Valentina grimaced. "Champagne. They took a case of it. Probably all they could carry. It's heavy. And they smashed the rest."

"Two hundred and fifty bottles, two hundred and twenty dollars per bottle," Carlos spat.

Fifty thousand dollars' worth of champagne. All gone.

"Damn. Sucks for you," Leon offered helpfully.

Valentina looked green.

"Do you have the security footage?" I asked.

A minute later, I watched three figures in dark hoodies with bandannas over their faces spray the security cameras with whipped cream, which they found in the fridge.

"We don't usually use canned whipped cream," Valentina said. "The client had specifically requested it for her bachelorette party. We didn't ask."

The sounds of champagne being smashed came from the screen. I glanced at Leon. He nodded.

I rewound the recording. "Look. They get through the window and they go straight to the fridge. They knew that the window would be unlocked and bypassed, and they knew right where the whipped cream was."

"What are you implying?" Carlos asked. His eyes bulged. "I know everyone who works here. I vouch for everyone who works here."

Humans dealt with risk by pretending it didn't exist. Even though thousands of people died every year in car accidents, we still got into our cars and drove every day. We built illusions of safety around ourselves and believed them or we would go insane.

A home was one of those vital illusions. It was our shelter, the place where we let our guard down. Nothing bad was supposed to happen to you in your house. When our warehouse was attacked by mercenaries, it felt like my world was cracked open. It made me feel weak and helpless.

Valentina and Carlos were feeling helpless now. The financial loss was crushing, but the violation of their kitchen was likely worse. This was a small business. The employees were probably more like family than hired help. They spent a lot of time together in this kitchen, making delicious food and beautiful cakes. Someone had smashed all those happy memories to pieces. The idea that one their own might have done it was too much.

"Are there any bottles left?" Leon asked.

Valentina reached under the counter and pulled a heavy bottle out. Leon grabbed the bottle by the neck and smashed it against the wall. The bottle held.

"Hey!" Carlos yelled.

I held up my hand. "We'll reimburse you."

It took Leon two more tries before the bottle finally broke.

Panting a little, he held the bottle out to me. "Two hundred, like this?"

I turned to Valentina. "If you're just kids breaking in to steal some wine, you'd grab a few bottles and get out. This took a lot of time and effort. The question is why."

"Yes, why? Why would anybody do this?" Valentina asked.

"Two possible reasons," I said. "First, they were covering up the sound of what they were doing, and second, they counted on you concentrating on the loss of the wine. Our contract with you specified that you were to call us immediately in case of any complications. Why didn't you call us?"

"We called the police," Carlos said.

"You don't understand," Valentina said, her face plum red now. "We came in and there were piles of glass on the floor. All this wine, the smell . . ."

And she had wanted to clean it up as soon as possible, to erase the desecration of their beautiful kitchen.

"It's misdirection." Leon nodded at the broken glass on the floor. "Smashed bottles, broken glass, expensive wine on the floor, everything smells, everything is stained and sticky. You see this and if nothing else appears disturbed, you just concentrate on cleaning things up."

I looked at Valentina and Carlos, and my insides tried to squeeze themselves into a tight painful ball. There were things I had to say now, harsh and unkind things, and I had to say them to two people who were already desperate and traumatized. I felt mean and shitty. But it was my job. I promised I would do it.

"You're in breach of contract," I said. "You were hired by House Rogan. This is House business. Normal rules do not apply here. We were crystal clear when we went over the contract with you. My sister and I sat at this table and read the contract to you paragraph by paragraph and you said you understood and you signed it. First, you failed to set the alarm."

Carlos sucked in a lungful of air, about to say something, but Valentina put her hand on his arm.

"Second, you failed to notify us of the break-in. The contract specifically spells out that we are to be informed in the event of any problems prior to any contact with law enforcement, unless it's a life-threatening emergency. Third, you cleaned up, destroying the evidence."

Nobody said anything.

Valentina bit her lip. "If you cancel everything now, we will be ruined."

I knew exactly what she was thinking. She was looking into the future and seeing the death of her business. And I was the person who decided if it lived or died. I had never wanted to teleport more in my entire life. If I could, I would have run away and pretended this never happened.

"Is there anything we can do to fix this?" Valentina asked.

"It depends," I said. "I would like access to your computer. I will be able to tell you more depending on what we find. Under the terms of our contract, I cannot compel you to grant me access. You can refuse."

"And if we do?" Carlos asked.

I raised my hands. "We walk away."

"Go ahead." Valentina waved at a desktop in the corner by a small desk.

I activated the recording function on my phone. "This is Catalina Baylor. Today is April 20th. I am here with Valentina Krueger, owner of Valentina's House Catering. May I have access to your business computer?"

"Yes."

"Thank you."

Leon headed for the desktop. His fingers flew over the keyboard. "Did you shut the computer down before you left?"

"Yes," Valentina said. She sounded like she expected us to hit her with a baseball bat. "We shut it off every night before we leave."

"What was the last thing you worked on?" Leon asked.

"Fishmonger list," Valentina said.

"Well," Leon said. "Somebody turned it back on at

the time of the break-in and accessed the Rogan Cake file."

Crap. I turned to Valentina and Carlos. "Can I have your cell phones, please? I don't need you to unlock them, I just want you to put them on the table over there. And not touch them, until I give them back to you."

"Oh my God." Valentina's eyes got big. "They tampered with the cake. But it's not even put together yet. We just started the sponges yesterday."

"Phones, please," Leon said. His tone was matter-of-fact, but there was something in the way he said it that communicated that disobeying him was a very bad idea.

Two phones landed on the metal table.

"I would like you to go to the pantry and review your inventory. Do not touch anything. If something looks wrong, if it has been moved, or the lid is not on just right, tell me immediately. Please keep the pantry door open, so I can see you."

The two bakers went into the pantry. I dialed Rogan's number. He answered on the second ring. "Yes?"

"I believe someone poisoned your wedding cake. How would you like me to proceed?"

IN HALF AN HOUR, Rogan's troops, assigned to Mrs. Rogan's house, arrived in two armored cars. New Braunfels was only half an hour from Mountain Rose, but it felt like it took them forever. I spent the time trying to figure out who might have wanted to poison Nevada's cake. Rogan and Nevada had made plenty of enemies when they stopped a conspiracy by several prominent Houses to seize power in Texas. Most of these enemies were dead or in jail.

When Primes killed someone in revenge, they wanted the whole world to know about it. They didn't delegate. They wanted to look into your eyes as their magic choked the life out of you. Poison just seemed so mundane. And, because we had just become a House, none of the Primes could legally attack us for the next three years.

Besides, a lot of Primes would be attending. The guest list read like the Powerful and Influential page on Herald. Whoever poisoned the cake would have killed members of Houston's magical elite. There would be no place for them to hide. It didn't feel like a politically or financially motivated attempt. It felt like hate. Blinding hate, so powerful, it made you forget about your own safety.

I had made a list of suspects. One name kept coming up. Someone who hated Rogan. Who was jealous, hateful, and reckless.

Rivera was the first one through the door. Behind him came a woman in the loose fatigues a lot of Rogan's employees wore. A baseball cap was pulled down tightly on her head. The rest of the crew secured the perimeter, spreading out through and outside of the bakery.

The woman took off her ball cap. She was about my age, redheaded, with skin so pale, it almost glowed. One of my grandfathers was black, and we weren't sure about the other. Both of my grandmothers were white, and all the genes mixed together gave me a naturally tan skin and dark brown hair. A lot of my friends were paler than me, but this girl had epic levels of paleness. It's like she didn't even know what the sun was. How did she survive in Texas?

"Runa Etterson of House Etterson, Magus Venenata." She stuck her hand out at me.

Venenata was Latin for poison. Runa was a poison mage and she was smiling at me and holding her hand out. She could probably poison me by just breathing in my direction.

"Catalina Baylor. Of House Baylor." I shook her hand.

She grinned at me. "Aha, took you a second. Don't worry, I only poison random strangers on Tuesdays."

"Today is Tuesday," Leon said.

"Oops. Well, that's okay. You told me your name, so we're not strangers. You should be safe." She turned to Leon. "But I don't know who you are. No promises."

"This is my cousin, Leon."

"Nice to meet you, Cousin Leon. So, where are the potentially poisoned goodies?"

I led her to the refrigerators and opened the doors. Tubs of frosting and fondant in every color filled the shelves. Runa rubbed her hands together.

"Come on, guys, don't just stand there. Grab a spoon and let's get busy."

Nobody said anything or moved.

"What? How did you think this worked? That I would wiggle my nose and sniff out the poison? If only. No, you eat it and if you die, I can say, 'Yes, it's been poisoned.'"

Rivera sighed. "Ma'am. Please take this seriously. According to the agreement between House Rogan and House Etterson . . ."

"Yes, yes. I've been stuck in the guardhouse on a chance someone at this wedding will get poisoned for the last two weeks. Let me have a little fun."

Runa raised her hands. A faint green mist spread from her, passed through the refrigerators, and dissipated. She stepped forward, took a tub of ice-white fondant out, opened it, pinched some fondant off, and popped it in her mouth. "Mmm, delicious cyanide. Old school. Histotoxic hypoxia on you, histotoxic hypoxia on your house, histotoxic hypoxia on your cow. Wait." She held her hand up. "What is this fishy aftertaste?"

Runa ate a little more and smacked her lips loudly. "It's on the tip of my tongue. Ooo. Tetrodotoxin. Sneaky. Cyanide would kill you in minutes, but if you happened to somehow take an antidote, tetrodotoxin would still get you."

Runa held out her hands. "Every tub in here is poisoned. All of the fondant. If the poisoner wanted to simply assassinate the happy couple, they could have used thallium. It is odorless, tasteless, lethal, and it takes several days to kick in. What this person did is about as subtle as taking a hammer and smashing the bride and groom on the head with it. You are looking for someone for whom Connor's and Nevada's death is deeply personal. This person wants to see them suffer and die. They will likely be in the wedding party or near it. They want to inflict pain and witness it so badly, they are willing to risk their personal safety. They can't wait to do it. There is glee in this and a horrible malice."

This aligned with everything I was thinking so far. I pulled up my main suspect and showed the tablet to Rivera and Leon. Rivera's eyes narrowed.

"Makes sense," he said.

A crazy grin tugged at Leon's mouth. "Oh, I hope so. I really hope so."

"Who is responsible for the fondant?" I asked.

"Jeremy," Carlos said. "But he's a good kid. He wouldn't do this."

Rivera spoke into his phone. "Bug, I need a full workup on Jeremy Wagner. Payments, debt history, any connection to Rogan or Baylor. I want to know where he was and what he was doing since Valentina's was hired for the wedding. Anything you can dig up."

We had done a background check on every employee. Jeremy Wagner had come back clean, which meant that either we were incompetent, or his darkness was well hidden. Trying to retrace Jeremy's steps in the last few days, even with Bug's talent, would take time. We didn't have time. Right now, in Mountain Rose, Mrs. Rogan could be serving the children poisoned lemonade.

I had to use my magic. I felt cold and nauseous and sticky, as if I had been poisoned. It was an awful feeling. My heart was hammering in my chest. I wanted to go somewhere alone and quiet, anywhere but here. I wanted this to be somebody else's problem.

They were going to poison my sister. And Rogan. And his mother. And all their friends, relatives, and children. Mia Rosa with her bedazzled unicorn. I could think of only one person who had that kind of hate.

"I will interview Jeremy."

Rivera startled. Leon frowned at me. "Are you sure?"

"Yes."

"The real target is the person who hired Jeremy," Rivera said.

"I'm aware of that. The background will take time and may not turn up anything. It's a simple matter of what would be quickest and produce the best results. If I ask him, he will tell me."

Rivera spoke slowly and deliberately. "If I wanted to poison someone by tampering with the wedding cake, I would watch the bakery to make sure the tampering was not discovered. The moment you question Jeremy, we will have to sit on him. If the poisoner suspects that we know about the cake, they will try again, and this time we may not find it in time. Tracing Jeremy's employer through Bug is cleaner and carries less risk."

"And what if Bug doesn't find anything?" Leon asked.

Whatever happened, my cousin was in my corner.

"If he doesn't find anything, then we squeeze Jeremy," Rivera said.

"I can question Jeremy and make sure he won't remember it."

Leon's eyebrows crept up.

"Are you sure?" Rivera asked.

I wasn't sure, but sooner or later I had to try it. It had to work. My sister's life depended on it.

"Yes. It's plausible that we would talk to all of the employees after the break-in."

"If Catalina says she can do it, she can do it," Leon said.

"Okay," Rivera said.

I turned to Valentina. "Please call in your employees. Let them know that there has been a burglary and they will be interviewed. Meanwhile, I need you to replace all of the fondant with an identical product. If Jeremy is in on it, he will not taste the fondant, because he knows it's lethal, so he'll have no way of knowing it was switched."

"Ahem," Runa said. "Or you could let me purify the fondant for you, no need to replace or dispose of anything."

"But will it be safe?" Valentina asked.

The smile vanished from Runa's face. Suddenly her expression turned cold and harsh. "Let me introduce myself again. Runa Etterson of House Etterson, *Prime* Venenata. I have walked into a house filled with sarin and after I was done, the family hiding upstairs in the safe room, walked out and made coffee for me in their kitchen. Mad Rogan trusts my House with the safety of the people who are most precious to him. If I say the fondant is safe to use, it's safe to use. Stand back please."

Runa pulled out chalk and began drawing an arcane circle on the floor.

Chapter 6

I SAT IN the small office on the other side of the building. Normally this room was used to meet with clients
and go over menus and cake books. Today there would
be questions about cakes, but they would have a different
flavor.

Rivera took his job as chief of security very seriously.
He and two of his guys wouldn't budge from their
position behind me. Runa perched on the chair, flipping
through a photo album filled with beautiful cakes, on
the off chance Jeremy tried to poison me.

Leon leaned on the table next to me. "Are you okay?"
he asked quietly.

"Yeah." I would have to use my magic with finesse.
The few times I'd actively used it required power. Finesse was entirely different.

When I was born, the nurse who helped deliver me

picked me up out of the crib by my mother's side and ran. They caught her before she made it off the floor, and when they took me away from her, she screamed and cried. In twenty years of nursing, she had never done anything like that. That woman lost her career because I was born with the kind of magic that made people love me.

She was the first but not the last. Over the years, there had been others. A dentist who examined my teeth tried to hide me in his office and then claimed that I ran away. I was two years old. The preschool teacher loaded me into her car and tried to run my mother over when she attempted to stop her. When we would go shopping, strangers would follow me as I rode in the cart and employees would try to give me things for free.

Other babies and toddlers were encouraged to be cute. I was taught to never draw attention to myself, not to smile at strangers, and not to make friends. If I liked another child, they would abandon everything to play with me. But soon playing wouldn't be enough. They would follow me, mesmerized, and then they would want a piece of me, a piece of my dress, a lock of my hair, some skin, maybe a finger. Once it started, I didn't know how to stop it. Only my family and my primary doctor were immune.

I was homeschooled until high school, when it became clear that I could control my power well enough to keep it from leaking. I had practiced controlling my magic since the moment I understood that I ruined lives. My talent was extremely rare, but I studied similar magics, I practiced arcane circles, and I read all about magic theory, but theory, by definition, wasn't practice.

I had experimented before on my sisters, because they were immune, and I had no way of knowing if anything I learned would actually work. Rivera shouldn't have bothered with the lecture. I needed him and his guys here. He knew what I could do. If I failed to control my power and besotted Jeremy snapped, they would pull him off me.

The door swung open and Jeremy Wagner walked in. Just like in his pictures, which I had reviewed when we vetted him, Jeremy was a tall, dark-haired Caucasian man in his midtwenties. He had one of those generic faces, neither ugly nor handsome, but overall pleasant. There was something soft and sheepish about his demeanor. He seemed like a timid man who knew he was timid and decided to use it to his advantage.

He should have been nervous, concerned at the very least, possibly defensive. Most people would have their guard up. Instead he looked slightly sleepy. It might have been because he'd spent the night breaking into the bakery, but his pictures confirmed that he always looked that way.

"Please sit down," I said.

"Hi." He sat and gave me a smile. Even the way he smiled at me reinforced the sheepishness, as if he were trying to say, "Boy, I'm a mess, but aren't I cute?"

"You are here because someone broke into the shop last night."

"Oh yeah? Did they take anything?"

When my magic was evaluated by a panel of Primes, the Keeper of Records, who registered the members of every House in Houston, had to come up with a name for my brand of power. He called me Siren. Most people thought of sirens as mermaids, but in the original myths, they had feathers and wings. I had wings too. Mesmerizing, beautiful wings that glittered with magic. Nobody ever saw them, except me, but when I opened them, people focused on me and forgot about everything else.

For most people using magic required conscious thought and effort. Like punching a bag or doing a push-up. They practiced and got stronger. For me, it was the opposite. Keeping my wings closed when I was around strangers was like always holding my breath. Opening them was effortless.

I didn't need my full power for Jeremy. I only need a tiny bit of it, so I let him see a bare hint of my feathers. He blinked and smiled at me.

I opened my mouth and my magic stretched forward, fused with my voice, and wound about him, an invisible thread that lured him in. The effort to hold back my power, only letting a tiny bit through, was exhausting.

"They smashed some wine bottles. Do you like wine, Jeremy?"

He was focused completely on me now. "I'm more of a beer guy. I like all kinds of beer. I like IPAs the best. You know, when you can really taste the hops. It's a real beer. It's like studying surrealism. You drink an IPA and there is nothing abstract or vague about it. It's citrus and hops . . ."

I had him. In the corner Runa sat up straighter and put her photo book down.

". . . a baseline against which all other beers should be compared. Like is it stronger than an IPA? Is it sweeter or less hoppy? Do you like beer? There is a great biergarten we can go to right now and I will buy you an IPA."

"Jeremy, are you good at decorating cakes?"

"I'm the best at decorating cakes. Better than people on tv." Jeremy's eyes went wide. "I watch *The Cake Tournament* and most of that shit is pure crap. I am a fucking wizard with fondant. If we had some fondant right now, I could really show you something."

"There is fondant in the bakery," I said.

"Oh no, we can't use that. It's poisoned."

Leon smiled.

"That's weird. Who poisoned it?"

Jeremy waved his hand. "My younger bro and two of his buddies from high school. That's not important. I did all the hard work. I set this up."

My voice wrapped around him, seductive and reassuring. "Wow, you must be very smart, Jeremy. Why would you set it up?"

"I never liked Primes. They act like they're so much

better than us. Oh, and this woman paid me a hundred grand in cash. I've got it buried in my backyard. I'm rich. I don't have to work here. You should let me take you out. We could go to South Padre."

I turned my tablet on and showed him the picture I had pulled up.

"That's her," he said. "Do you know her? Did she give you money? I would give you money. I've got money."

"Do you know how she's getting into the wedding?" I asked.

"Nah. She just gave me a bunch of syringes with stuff in them and said to inject the fondant. And she told me not to poke myself with them and to wear plastic gloves." He rolled his eyes. "Duh, like I'm stupid."

Now came the most difficult part.

I opened my mouth and sang. The words didn't matter, only the magic did. Jeremy listened, his jaw hanging slack. The magic wrapped around him, like a glittering veil, and he began to sing with me. "Baa baa black sheep, have you any wool, yes sir, yes sir, three bags full . . ."

I fell silent and gently untangled my magic from him, as it whispered into his mind. *Forget, forget, forget.*

His head drooped, his chin falling to his chest. He pitched forward slowly. His stomach touched the table. Jeremy jerked awake. He blinked at me, his eyes looking wild.

"They smashed some wine bottles," I said. "Do you like wine, Jeremy?"

"I'm more of a beer guy."

"Did you have anything to do with the break-in?" I asked him.

"Nope. It's a shame though. I mean who would be dumb enough to break into a bakery?"

"Where were you last night between one and two?" I was so tired now. My voice was shaking.

"I was home. My brother will vouch for me. We stayed up playing video games."

"Okay, Jeremy, you're free to go."

"Great." He got up and offered me his hand. I shook it. His handshake was limp. "Great to meet you." He walked out.

Nobody said anything. Rivera stared at his phone. Leon was grinning at me like a lunatic and holding two thumbs up.

Rivera looked up. "Okay, he went into the kitchen."

"Well, that was something else," Runa said.

A wild thought occurred to me. I stuck my hand out. "Catalina Baylor, of House Baylor, Prime Siren."

Runa looked at my hand, took it carefully, and shook it. "Stay out of my head."

"Don't poison anybody I know, and I will."

"Is the memory loss permanent?" Rivera asked.

"I don't know," I said.

"We're going to watch him," Rivera said. "My guess is he told you everything he knows, and she's too smart to give him anything that could lead us to her. We're going to proceed as if we bought the teenager wine story.

We're going to put guards here, because it's expected."

"If she wants to get into the wedding, it will have to be the waitstaff," I said.

Rivera nodded. "That seems most likely."

Leon stirred. "Carlos will be a problem. If he suspects Jeremy did this, he won't be able to control himself."

Rivera smiled. "We will tell him that he passed with flying colors. You already got them to sign the NDA."

Rogan had emailed me a nondisclosure agreement that forbade Valentina and Carlos to even mention the word *poison* for the next two weeks. If they broke this agreement, we would immediately terminate our contract. If they managed to stick to it, Rogan would pay for the smashed wine bottles. I had to explain to them in excruciating detail that they, their online communications, and their phone calls would be monitored until after the wedding. It made me feel like a corporate gangster. Like I had come into their shop and smashed it demanding protection money, but it was all legal and binding.

"I think I would like to go now," I told Leon.

LEON DROVE, WHILE I fought my way through my text messages. Mrs. Rogan wanted to know if there was any progress on finding Sealight. There wasn't, so I told her we were working on it. Rogan wanted to know if I was okay. I wasn't, so I told him I was fine. Mom wanted to know if we were coming home for dinner. We were, and I said yes. Arabella wanted to know if she could put a piece of duct tape over Nevada's mouth and fingers, so she would stop changing the stupid wedding. I told her no. I got a very nice email from Mia Rosa typed by her mother, which thanked me for the bedazzler. Which was awesome. Someone had asked me for something, I did it, and they were happy and said thank you.

The last text was from Bern. "Where are you?"

"In the car, with Leon."

"Are you going back to Mountain Rose?"

"Yes, but only for a minute." I needed to make sure they finished the tent like they were supposed to.

"I need you to find a safe place to pull over. I'm sending you some footage you need to see before you get there."

What? "Send it. I'll just look at it while Leon is driving."

"No, I need you to pull over."

I sighed. "Your brother is being weird."

"And this is news how?"

"Can you take the next exit and find a good spot to pull over?"

Two minutes later, Leon pulled over from 281 into a gas station lot and parked. I sent Bern a text. My email dinged, and I started the download on my phone. It was taking forever.

"That was awesome back there," Leon said. "I didn't know you could do that."

"I didn't know I could either."

"Does it feel good when you use your magic?"

"It feels good to not hide it."

If we weren't in a parking lot in public, I would open my wings and just rest. I was even afraid to do it while we were driving. I couldn't take a chance on someone fixating on me and wrecking their car.

"He was going to poison all of us, Leon. When I think about it, it kind of freaks me out. Anybody, *everybody* who ate that cake would have died. Little kids would have died. And he didn't care. I could tell when he was talking, that part of it was the money but not all of it. He did it because he hates us. He doesn't even know us. He didn't feel bad about it, Leon—he was proud of it."

Leon leaned back in his seat. "Everybody in our family has magic. Aunt Penelope, Grandma Frida, you, your sisters, Bern . . . I thought I didn't have magic. I thought I was a dud. I used to climb to the top of the warehouse. There is a way to get to the roof from the attic. I would walk on the edge of the roof."

"Why in the world would you do that?"

"I thought maybe if I got scared enough, my powers would come out." Leon grimaced. "You can practice and get good at sports. You can study and get good grades. But with magic, you have it or you don't. That's it. And it's so fucking unfair. Here you are, and an accident of birth, something in your DNA that you have no control over, decides, before you're even born, how your life is going to go."

I couldn't remember a time when I didn't have magic. It was this scary thing that ruled my life. I had so much guilt wrapped up in it. I never told Leon about it, because I knew he would have given up half of his life for some of that power.

"But you didn't poison people," I said.

"Who would I poison? You're my family. I love you. I wouldn't even poison Mom if she showed back up. I did hate her, you know. Still do. First, if she had slept with Bern's dad instead of whoever my dad was, I would have had magic. Some magic. Second, she is a piss-poor mom."

I tried to look for the best things in people. There was nothing good about Aunt Gisele. I used to think that she was just misunderstood but then she showed up and wrecked our life, and now I hated her too.

"Jeremy is a scumbag," Leon said. "He's too stupid to realize he isn't smart. But he sees all the Primes in the news and on Herald, and he envies them. The jealousy is eating him alive. Once the wedding is over, Rivera will make sure he's turned over to the proper authorities."

Rogan could make Jeremy disappear, but he wouldn't. I once asked Nevada about things like that and she said that being a House meant projecting a show of strength. If someone like Jeremy attacked a House, they would want to make a very public example of him.

The file downloaded. I tapped it. The feed from one of the hummingbird cameras filled the screen. Xavier was walking toward his cousins. I turned the sound up.

Adriana, the tall blonde, took a step toward Xavier, her face stamped with anger. Spanish words flew out. "Why are you doing this? She is a nice girl. Leave her alone."

They were talking about me.

"Shut the fuck up," Xavier said.

Elba giggled from her spot on the fountain, the gold bracelets on her tan arms sliding back and forth as she waved her hands.

"I mean it." Adriana crossed the space between them and got in his face. "Leave Catalina alone. She is working really hard. She doesn't know you're a snake. Find someone else to screw around with."

Xavier crossed his arms. Adriana was tall, but he was taller by at least four inches. "Or what? What are you going to do? Let me tell you what you will do: nothing. You've been doing nothing. None of you are doing anything about this wedding. He's going to marry that bitch."

My heart hammered in my chest. My cheeks were getting hot. Adriana was right. He was a snake. And I almost let him bite me.

"What do you care?" Samanta, the one with curly dark hair, said. "Let him get married."

He turned toward her. "If you stopped shoving food

in your mouth long enough to think, you'd figure it out. You want to explain it to her, Elba?"

"Rogan leads a dangerous life," Elba said. "He has powerful enemies. Think about it—he's old, like thirty something, and this is the first time he tried to marry someone. His mom is in a wheelchair because people kept trying to kill his dad. On top of that, everyone knows he's a sicko. Then this bitch, a complete nobody, shows up and now he's marrying her without a prenup."

"Exactly," Xavier jumped in. "He dies one day after the wedding, she gets everything, and we get nothing. Let me explain it to you in small words, so you can understand. Our grandparents are drawing money from family investments. They are not getting that much, one-two mil a year each. Our parents have to work. By the time the grandparents die off, and our parents start drawing their share, they will be getting even less money, because there are more of them. We'll have to work and when it's our turn, there might not be anything left over. You know who has money?"

"Rogan," Elba said. "A nice pretty billion."

"Rogan will get himself killed sooner or later. My dad says he made a lot of powerful enemies this last year. Arrosa is old. All we have to do is wait." Xavier snapped his fingers. "And we'll inherit. But for that to happen there needs to be no wife and no heir."

"What are you going to do, Xavier?" Adriana sneered at him. "Even if you break up the wedding, are you going to follow him around with a rubber to make sure he doesn't make any kids?"

"That will be later. Right now, we have a more pressing issue. He is marrying that bitch."

"They are Primes," Samanta shot back.

"Yeah, last time I checked, Xavier, you weren't a Prime." Adriana crossed her arms.

"Neither are you," Xavier said. "I looked up their records and they just became a House this year. She's a truthseeker, there is a pattern mage, but everybody else's records are sealed. They are upstarts. If they had useful magic, they would've announced it. What kind of Prime doesn't disclose their magic? Trust me, they're trash. Have you seen Catalina scurrying around with her tablet, like a mouse with a piece of old cheese? She's a Prime? Please. A Prime geek. She knows she doesn't belong here. She told me she feels 'uncomfortable.' She'll feel uncomfortable when I kick her and her sister off the grounds."

I saw red. I actually saw red, as if someone suddenly jerked a translucent red curtain closed in front of me.

"I'm going to shove a gun up his ass sideways," Leon snarled.

Xavier paced back and forth. "All that's required of you is to keep your mouths shut and stay out of my way, while I romance that rat. She's got the entire wedding and probably half her family secrets on that tablet she carries with her. I'm going to get that tablet."

"You really are an asshole," Adriana said.

"Don't worry," Xavier said. "Even though great-grandfather kicked your mom out of the family for being a lesbo, you and I can work something out when we inherit."

"Xavier!" Samanta glared at him.

Elba grinned. "Don't be jealous. If I were you, I would be doing everything I could to help us. The way Lucian sleeps around, you'll have to share your inheritance with an army of bastards."

"Ugh!" Adriana spun and walked away. Samanta looked after her, glanced at Xavier and Elba, and hurried after Adriana.

"Don't worry," Elba said. "Samanta is a coward, and Adriana won't say anything. She's bought Isabella's pills off me a couple of times. She's got 'anxiety' and if her mom finds out, she'll skin her alive."

Xavier grimaced. "Good, keep them under control and I'll handle the rest."

The recording stopped.

"I'll fucking kill him." Leon growled. "I'll drown him in that damn fountain and then I'll CPR him back and drown him again."

A pit had opened in my stomach. I tasted acid on my tongue and swallowed it back down. Hot tears wet my cheeks, burning the skin. It was as if I had been poisoned and my body was desperately trying to expel it.

"Don't cry, Catalina—he's not worth it. Don't let him make you sad." Leon hovered next to me. "Please don't cry. I'll make it okay somehow. Just don't cry, or I might cry with you, and then you'll tell everybody, and I'll be embarrassed. Do you need tissues? I have tissues."

He grabbed a box of tissues from the backseat and thrust them in my hands. "Don't be sad."

"I'm not sad," I ground through clenched teeth. "I'm angry."

Leon blinked. "You don't get angry."

I turned and looked at him. He shied back.

"That waste of space actually thinks that he has a chance against us. He thinks that I'm so flattered that he paid attention to me for ten minutes that I'll just do whatever he wants. He thinks he dazzled me. That arrogant prick!"

Leon flinched.

"And their brilliant plan! They'll get ahold of my tablet, because that's where we keep all our family's deep shameful secrets."

"Do we have those?" Leon asked.

"No, but they do, and I will find every last one of them. They think they can break up the wedding, so in some distant future Rogan will die alone. I can't even! This is the dumbest thing I ever heard. It's like a tv movie for tweeners."

"Yes, that is some *Parent Trap* level shit, right there."

"It's something a twelve-year-old would come up with. Xavier is an adult! Elba is sixteen years old. They can't take care of themselves, they're petulant, they're immature, they don't know basic things, they're dumb, and their magic is nowhere near ours. Where does this superior attitude come from exactly?"

Leon started the car and locked the doors. "Okay," he said in a soothing voice. "Your face is turning purple and I've never seen it do that before. I really think we should just go home."

"No, we're going back to Mountain Rose and I will feed him this tablet."

"Well, I'm driving so I say we're going home."

"Leon!"

"Just keep in mind," Leon said, merging onto the highway, "I'm your cousin and you love me. If you attack me while I'm driving, we will both die and then he wins. Don't let him win, Catalina."

I SAT IN the kitchen, going through the background files. Leon had taken off for his room and a shower. Bern was working in the computer room we called Hut of Evil. It was just me, Arabella, Mom, and Grandma Frida in the kitchen.

I had looked at the files some yesterday, but they were a mile long, and I didn't review them as thoroughly as I needed to. Thanks to Xavier's little rant, I had some nice suspects.

I focused on Mikel, who managed Ramírez Capital, and was the husband of Maria of many cocktails, white clothes, and loud gold jewelry and father to Elba, who was a vicious little bitch. When Xavier put on his little performance for me as we walked by the fountain and he told Elba off, he said something about Mikel paying off the house staff. On the way back to the warehouse, I had scoured his file. On paper, Mikel drew a salary equivalent to one point four million dollars. He had no other significant sources of income. Maria spent money at an alarming rate. They lived in a seven-million-dollar mansion; they had a second home in Barcelona, valued at five million; they owned four luxury cars, totaling over eight hundred thousand dollars; a yacht; and they showed no signs of slowing down. Where was all the money coming from?

I had asked Bug to comb through his financial statements and to let me know as soon as he found something.

Lucian de Baldivia was the next on my list. He was married to June, but it seemed everyone in the family knew he was having affairs. I'd been tracking cheaters down for years and I knew that affairs weren't free. They left a trail. Hotels, gifts, dates, luxury getaways disguised as work conferences or conventions, more gifts, this time to the wronged spouse. Rogan's files listed twenty-three women Lucian had slept with since marrying June twenty years ago, and twelve of these relationships were long-term affairs. Every couple of years he got the itch and found someone to scratch it. His last affair ended eighteen months ago. He was about due for a new one, and the Sealight would make a pretty present.

There was still Paul Sarmiento, the boy toy, who appeared to have materialized out of thin air. He was a mystery: nobody knew him, nobody knew how Ane knew him, and nobody knew what he did. Two hundred and fifty thousand dollars might not be a huge windfall for the Ramírez and de Baldivias, but it was an attractive prize for the average thief . . .

Arabella moaned and dramatically slammed her head on the table.

Mom and Grandma Frida put down their utensils and clapped.

"I've had it," my sister announced. "She is not getting those damn lilacs and that's final."

"If she wants lilacs, just let her have lilacs. What's the harm?" Grandma Frida asked.

"Her colors scheme is sage, pink, and white. Blue is going to clash with it. It's going to be ugly. The bouquet will be in all the important photographs and everybody is going to notice how ugly it looks. You don't understand, Grandma. People on Herald are vicious. I don't want Nevada to be torn apart. They're going to be mean. They're jealous. Nobody wants to hear a story about a beautiful wedding, but everyone is going to make fun of a Prime bride who is marrying a billionaire but couldn't afford to coordinate her bouquet. No!"

"Since when do we care what people on Herald think?" Mom asked.

"Since we became a House and everyone thinks we're country bumpkins." Arabella spun to me. "Catalina, tell them."

Everyone looked at me.

"Fuck Herald," I said.

Grandma Frida dropped her fork.

"Fuck Primes, fuck their paparazzi, and if Nevada wants lilacs, she should have all the lilacs ever. I will buy the damn lilacs myself, with my own money." I took my tablet and walked out.

Behind me, Arabella said, "Mom?"

"I think your sister is a little stressed out," Mom said.

I made a left turn to another hallway and walked to the Hut of Evil. When we sold our house to pay for Dad's medical treatment and moved into the warehouse, the original plan was to set it up as homelike as possible. But instead we just threw walls up wherever they were needed and ended up with some unusual spots. To a stranger, our layout wouldn't make much sense but to us, it worked great. The Hut of Evil was one of those odd places. It was a small room inside a larger space complete with the door and a roof and raised off the ground to accommodate all the cables and the cooling. I had to walk up three steps to get in.

The temperature inside was at least five degrees cooler than in the rest of the house. Bern sat in his usual seat in front of three monitors. I took a seat in Leon's chair.

"Rough day," Bern said.

"They lie, and cheat, and steal. And they think they're better than us, because we work, and we don't have as much money. This is the kind of family Nevada is marrying into."

"Nevada is marrying Rogan. I like Rogan. I like Mrs. Rogan too, and the East Wing side of the family seem decent. Look, most of them will go back to Europe after this, and we will never, ever see them again. We just have to get through the wedding."

"No, Nevada has to get through the wedding. We have to catch a thief and prevent mass murder at the wedding ceremony. Have you seen them doing anything weird? Something that could help us find the Sealight or whoever took it?"

Bern hesitated. "Well, not sure if it's related but you gotta see this. Hang on."

His fingers flew across the keyboard and an image appeared on the middle screen, a table on a patio, flanked by some chairs. The picturesque shrubs rustled, and a tall, lanky man stepped out of them, like some kind of jungle explorer emerging from the bush. Mikel Ramírez adjusted his glasses, looked around, and took off down a path, away from the building into the orchard.

"Keep watching," Bern said.

A long minute crept by.

Maria Ramírez stomped into frame, her chunky heels making clicking noises on the patio. A faint green smudge stained her white dress. There was a twig in her bleached blond hair. She was holding a martini glass in her hand. She took off her sunglasses, paused, like a hound finding the scent, and took off in the direction her husband had fled.

I put my hand over my mouth and shook my head. "This is just bizarre."

"She chases him like this, all over the house." Bern turned his blond head and looked at me. "At lunch, he excused himself from the table, and never came back. I think he crawled out of a window because neither of the exit cameras caught him, and then he was outside. He could have stolen the Sealight. He's pretty good at sneaking around."

"Yes, but he's a lousy telekinetic, barely an Average, and everything in his file says he's desperate for his father's approval, so it's unlikely he is hiding his power. He wouldn't be able to lift the wall. What about Paul Sarmiento?"

Bern tapped a quick sequence on the keys. Ane and Paul came into view. They sat in the soft chairs overlooking the distant hills. Paul reached over to the table, lifted the small kettle, and poured Ane a cup of tea.

"They are joined at the hip," Bern said. "If he stole the Sealight, she would have helped him, because I never see them apart for more than ten minutes. Also, most of them have used their powers since I started watching them. They levitate something minor or open a door with a wave of their hand. I'll double-check on this, but so far, he's done nothing. I don't think he's telekinetic."

In other words, we still had nothing.

"Will you be here tomorrow?"

"Yes," Bern said. "Why?"

"I'm going to poke this snake nest with a stick and I might need a lot of help."

"I'll be here," Bern promised. "Catalina, don't let this get personal. Let's find the jewel, catch the poisoner, and be done with them. What they think of us doesn't matter. This is an investigation just like any other. They are suspects. You only interact with them to get to your objective."

"I know."

We sat together in a comfortable silence, watching Lucian schmooze his father-in-law over some whiskey and cigars.

"Did you like him?" Bern asked.

"Not that much." Not as much as I had liked Alessandro Sagredo. Walking with Xavier had been nice, before I realized he was a two-faced scumbag, but it was nothing special. But when I saw Alessandro, I wanted to snap my wings open as far as they could go and dazzle him with everything I had, so he would be mine forever. I liked him so much, I had to let him go.

Chapter 7

IT WAS ALMOST brunch time, and I was walking through the garden of Mountain Rose, carrying a mimosa in each hand.

"*Turn to your right ahead,*" Bern said into my earpiece.

I turned and stopped at the neat little table with two chairs. The grounds were full of these little nooks, pretty places to sit and enjoy the outdoors. I turned toward the path and concentrated, letting just a little of my magic through. It came sluggishly. I was still tired from yesterday. My books said I would get better with practice. I tried not to think about how I would get that practice.

"*Incoming in three, two, one.*"

Maria Ramírez stumbled onto the path. She wore a white sheath dress that had a modest neckline but left her tan shoulders and arms bare. A thick gold chain hung from her neck and a matching cuff bracelet encircled her forearm.

I gave her a peek at my feathers and cast my shiny magic lure with my voice. "Would you care for a mimosa?"

Maria froze. Her expression relaxed and then she started toward me. "I would love one."

We sat at the table and sipped our mimosas.

"It's peaceful here," Maria said. "It's nice."

"It is nice," I said, saturating my words with more magic.

"Have you seen my husband?" Maria asked. "He would like it here."

"No. Tell me about your husband. What kind of man is he?"

"He's gentle and smart. And I love him so much. That's why it hurts so much when he betrays me." Tears welled up in Maria's eyes. "He betrays me with men. I can't compete with that. I can be prettier, I can be thinner, but I can't be a man. And that's what he likes."

Oh God. "How do you know he likes men?"

"He had a secretary and I would catch them sneaking off together. When I would find them, all conversation stopped. And then the secretary was fired, but Mikel paid him five hundred thousand dollars. I saw the record of the payment in his office. Then there was the gardener. I would see them meet when they thought I wouldn't notice. They would pass each other pieces of paper like children in school. Love letters."

"Have you read one?"

"No."

Somehow, I doubted folded pieces of paper equaled love letters. Drugs would be a much better explanation.

"And now he's doing it again. Do you know who he is doing it with?" She leaned toward me. "Lucian. My husband is having an affair with Lucian. I saw Mikel leave in the middle of the night to meet with him."

Maria gulped the rest of her mimosa. "I must find him." Her eyes widened, her lower lip trembled. She looked panicked. All of her emotions were focused on Mikel. I wouldn't get much out of her and it would be cruel to try.

"I think he went down that way." I pointed down the path and pulled my magic back.

Maria jumped up and headed down the path without looking back.

None of that made any sense. If Lucian was bisexual, he would have had affairs with men as well as women. Lucian had a voracious appetite and he denied himself nothing. If he'd wanted men, he would have had men and there was no record of any male companions.

I texted Rogan. "Sorry to interrupt. Do you know why Mikel paid a large bonus to his secretary after firing him? There is nothing in the files."

"No, I don't but ask my mother."

I texted Mrs. Rogan the same question. A grey bubble let me know she was typing the answer. It was taking her a while. I drummed my fingers on the table and drank a little more of my mimosa.

"That wasn't a secretary, dear. That was Angel. He is what people of my generation refer to as an illicit love child. Mikel had some wild days and managed to father a child at sixteen. The family compensated the mother well, but when Angel grew up, he wanted a relationship with his father. He's a sweet boy, but it didn't work out. Mikel wasn't what Angel was hoping for. Any progress on Sealight?"

"Not yet and thank you."

"You have my full confidence."

The phone chimed. Mrs. Rogan sent me a selfie of her and Mia Rosa in Mrs. Rogan's office. They were giving me the V for victory with their fingers.

If Lucian and Mikel weren't having an affair, why was Mikel sneaking out to meet him?

A thought occurred to me. "Bern, can you send a text message but make it appear to come from someone else?"

"Yes. Whose number do you want me to spoof?"

"I'll tell you when I get home." This will work better

if I wasn't here. They would let their guard down if all of us were gone.

I couldn't leave yet. I was due to meet with Paul Sarmiento in ten minutes. I had asked Mrs. Rogan to set the meeting up for me, so Paul wouldn't have any excuses to duck me.

"That was impressive," a man said.

I glanced up. Paul was leaning against a tree.

"Are you planning to do that to me?" he asked.

I FACED PAUL. He had caught me using my magic. He knew my secret. Normally I would've tried to escape the confrontation. But something happened in the past few days, somewhere between the poisoned cake and Xavier calling me a mouse. It seared the shyness out of me.

One time our parents took us for a winter vacation in Colorado. We skied and rode sleighs all day and I had the most fun my eight-year-old self could remember. On the evening before we were supposed to go home, I snuck out of our cabin at dusk and rode my sleigh down the hill into the woods. It was so pretty, snow was falling softly, and for a while I wandered around. Then the sun had set, the wind picked up, and it went from magical to being scary. The snow had covered my tracks and I didn't know where to go. I tried calling but nobody came. The cold was biting at my face, and I realized I had to save myself. I picked a direction and I walked. After a while, I couldn't feel my feet or my fingertips. It was so cold, and it hurt so much, that eventually I got used to it. I accepted it and got numb. I just kept walking through the pain, until my dad found me and carried me back to the cabin.

That's what it was like now. Bad, uncomfortable things kept happening, one after the other. Any one of them would have made me panic on its own, but all of them together made me numb. I had to get out of this forest. I had accepted that it wouldn't be easy or pleasant.

I looked at Paul and asked, "Are you going to force me to do that to you or would you prefer to sit down and talk?"

He walked over and took a seat at the table. "How can I help you?"

"I have a problem. According to every background check we've run, you don't exist. You have no driver's license, your fingerprints are not in any of the databases, and the documents that follow most people through life, like birth certificates, diplomas, and résumés, simply can't be found. So, I have two questions: Who are you and why are you here?"

"And if I refuse to answer?"

"I'm afraid I'll have to compel you to. We've had some complications and the safety of the wedding guests is at stake."

"I don't think you are afraid at all."

Paul reached into his pocket, took out a wallet, and pulled a business card out. He slid it across the table to me. It was a pale blue card with two words embossed on it in dark blue—Wishing Well. Under the words was an address located in Seattle, with a phone number.

"My name is Lance Gibson. I'm an employee of the Wishing Well. Our corporate headquarters are in Japan, but I work out of the Seattle office. Ane is one of my clients."

There was no tactful way to ask the next question. "Are you an escort?"

"I'm not a prostitute, but, in a manner of speaking, I am Ane's escort. Our company specializes in wish fulfillment of a very specific nature. Have you ever felt that you are missing an important person in your life?"

I missed my dad every day. "I don't understand. Is it like the boyfriend experience?"

"It can be but typically it isn't." Lance steepled his fingers. "People come to us because there is a hole in their lives. For example, suppose a father abandons his wife and their young child. The wife divorces him. The child needs a father, yet she can't bring herself to enter another relationship. She might come to us and for a fee, one of us will become her divorced spouse for her child."

"So, you impersonate people? Like an actor?"

"Exactly like that. However, an actor assumes a different persona only for a short time, while we may do it for years. A couple hired me, because they have a daughter who is suffering from lupus. At the time, she was eight years old. She adored her older brother, who was fifteen years her senior. He was a remarkable individual, gifted, compassionate, and adventurous. Due to the nature of his charitable work, he traveled and always made time to call or email his little sister. One day the emails stopped. He died in a conflict in Belize. Her parents were terrified that the news would kill her. So, little by little, they replaced his photographs with mine. We started with emails, then phone calls, and then one day, her brother walked through the door. I'm there for every birthday. I'm the person she calls when she has problems at school or with her parents. This summer I'm taking her on a college tour."

"But you're not her brother."

Lance smiled. "No. But I'm fulfilling his role."

I wasn't sure what to think about that. "Will you ever tell her?"

"No. That is forbidden. Her parents can tell her, if and when they choose. Perhaps, when she no longer needs a brother, I will make a graceful exit. A plane crash, a skydiving accident. But for now, I'm there to provide a shoulder to lean on and the unconditional love and kindness one would expect from an older sibling."

"So, what are you to Ane?"

"Ane is single by choice. She enjoys being single. She was pressured into her marriage, and after her husband died, she was pressured again to remarry. Instead she hired me. Our relationship is not sexual. I escort her to family events and to vacations, I take care of her during these outings in a way a loving partner would be expected to take care of her, and on occasion, I act as her bodyguard. My services come with a guarantee a real relationship can't provide. I will never embarrass her. I will never get drunk, cause a scene, cheat on her, attempt to steal from her or coerce her into a course of action beneficial to myself, all of the things she had experienced in her prior relationships. Ane is in complete control. She engages my services as she wishes and can terminate our business relationship at any time."

"Does it bother you that people think you're a gigolo?"

Lance smiled again. "Why would I care what anybody but Ane thinks of me? The needs of my client are the only thing that matters. I'm paid to anticipate complications and smooth them over, which is why I'm talking to you now. I have emailed my credentials to Mr. Rivera, whom I understand to be in charge of security. You will find all of the necessary documents enclosed. Am I free to go, Ms. Baylor?"

Nobody had ever asked me that before. "Yes."

Lance rose and walked away.

"Did you get all that?" I asked Bern.

"*Yeah, I got it.*"

"I am coming home," I told him. "I think I've had enough for today."

I TEXTED TROY, one of Rogan's guys. Bern and I had decided that we should keep Leon as far away from

Xavier as was humanly possible, so Troy was my battle buddy for the day. He would get the car.

I started down the path that brought me to the courtyard. In the center, by the fountain, Xavier and Raul, one of Rogan's cousins from East Wing, sparred with rapiers. Mrs. Rogan and other adults were watching from the shade of the porch. The gaggle of teenagers surrounding them alternated between shouting encouragement and pretending to be bored.

Great. I would have to walk past them to my car. I started moving, hoping nobody would notice me.

"Catalina!" Xavier jogged toward me. The circle of kids parted to let him pass. People were catcalling.

I did my absolute best to ignore him. It was that or punch him in the throat. Usually people aimed for the face, because that's what you saw in movies and tv, but I grew up in a family of veterans. A punch to the throat didn't hurt your hand and it disabled your opponent.

Xavier ran ahead of me and blocked my way. He was holding two rapiers and offered me one. "Let's spar. It will be fun."

Oh, you moron. You colossal moron. If only you knew.

"Xavier!" Raul called. "Are we doing this or what?"

"Come on," Xavier said. "I'll show you."

"I don't know how, and I have things to do." Everybody was looking at me. It was like some kind of nightmare, but it was real and it was happening right now.

"Come on," he repeated. "Don't be an old lady."

I was so angry that my hands shook. This was the

worst-case scenario. The whole family was there, all the kids, and all the adults, and just me without anyone on my side.

Xavier waved the rapier in front of me.

Something in me snapped. I took it from him and marched into the circle.

Raul bowed and stepped aside. Xavier took position opposite me and slid into a stance. He probably had fencing lessons in whatever school he went to. I had no lessons, but I had a lot of hate. I had no idea what the point of this was, besides embarrassing me.

"First thing you do is get into *en garde* position. Like this. Turn your lead foot forward, bend your knees, make sure your knees are over your toes."

I just stood sideways, the way I always stood, when we practiced self-defense.

"Bend your knees," Xavier said.

Someone giggled.

"Are we going to fight or are you going to talk all day?" I asked.

The kids oohed. Raul gave me a thumbs-up.

"I'll go easy on you," Xavier said. "I'm going to lunge—try to parry."

The anger and my magic fused together. The world shrank down to just Xavier and me. The sword felt light and flexible in my hand, an extension of me, almost like an arm. I held it in front of me pointing at his midsection.

He lunged.

I shied out of his way and drove the blunted point of the rapier into his ribs on his left.

"Touché," someone screamed.

Xavier jerked back, anger flickering across his face. "I let you have that one. Are you ready?"

"Are you?"

He attacked. I didn't know how, but I knew exactly where he would strike. It felt like the sword itself guided me out of the way. I sidestepped and brought my sword with all my strength on top of his blade, knocking it out of his hand.

Xavier stared at me.

"You weren't ready," I said. "Your sword is over there. Are you supposed to be good at this?"

Xavier snatched his rapier up. His face was red now. He bared his teeth and lunged. I saw it, as if we were both underwater, the point of his rapier aiming straight for my unprotected face. Somehow I knew there was no time to back up, so I went forward instead, sliding my rapier against his, trying to force it to my right. We collided. The flat of his blade slid against mine, all the way to the guard, and suddenly our faces were very close.

Xavier's eyes were crazy.

He smashed his forehead into my face. I shied back, but not far or fast enough. Dark circles burst in front of my eyes. It hurt. It really hurt.

Raul was running toward us, and so was Adrianna. Xavier shoved me back. Something slammed into him from the right, knocking him aside like he weighed nothing.

The ground under my feet trembled and a terrible voice sounded from everywhere at once. *"Enough."*

Adrianna put her arms around me. "Are you okay?"

I blinked trying to clear the tears from my face. Xavier was sprawled on the ground two dozen yards away, a shocked look on his face. A heavy outdoor cushion pinned him in place. He was struggling to lift it off, his arms shaking with the strain. He should've been able to push it off of him, but it trapped him like it was made of cement.

The courtyard was completely silent. I turned and saw Mrs. Rogan on the porch. Magic emanated from her, like an invisible corona. I couldn't see it, but I felt it and the power in her took my breath away. It was like standing in the eye of a catastrophic storm. You couldn't see the wind, but you could feel it all around you, and if you took a step, it would rip you apart. I couldn't move, I couldn't speak. I just stood there, feeling the terror roll over me in icy waves.

Behind her, her three older siblings and their children looked outraged. The West Wing crowd didn't share the indignation. Markel and Zorion were sneering; Lucian raised his eyebrows, amused; Mikel and Maria looked alarmed; Eva, Xavier's mother, glared at Mrs. Rogan, and Iker, Xavier's father, wore a completely flat expression. The line splitting the family down the middle was never so clear.

Mrs. Rogan turned her head and stared at Eva. Her magic turned with her and stared at Eva, too, like an ancient dragon noticing a trespasser.

Eva looked at her feet. Her bottom lip trembled.

Iker stepped in front of his wife and bowed his head. "Our sincerest apologies. He is young and stupid. We meant no disrespect."

Mrs. Rogan spoke, and her voice reverberated through me, pulsing in my bones. The water in the fountain shook. "Take him to your rooms. He does not come out unless I call for him."

Iker strode to his son. The cushion lifted on its own and moved back to the outdoor sofa on the porch. Nobody moved to help Iker. He grabbed Xavier by his right shoulder and hauled him upright.

"Are you all right, dear?" Mrs. Rogan asked.

The dragon was looking at me. I had to say something, and it was so hard. "Yes, ma'am."

"I am so very sorry," Mrs. Rogan said. "Please forgive me."

I wanted to fall through the ground and keep falling until I was on the other side of the world. "It's okay. I'm fine, everything is fine. It's all good." I clicked my teeth shut before any more rambling nonsense came out.

"Very well. I think I will retire to my office. I've had all the excitement I could stand." The dragon folded her wings collapsing back, and Mrs. Rogan turned her wheelchair and rolled back into the house.

I turned and fled toward the gate as fast as I could. A

familiar Honda Element drove through the gates toward me, Troy behind the wheel. I almost ran. The Honda stopped, and I jumped into the passenger seat. Troy was looking at my hand and I realized I was still clutching the stupid rapier. There was blood on the blade. I must have cut Xavier somehow.

"What the hell happened?" Troy asked.

"Too complicated. Could you please just drive?"

Troy turned the car around and drove out of Mountain Rose.

"What took you so long?" I asked.

"We found Sealight," he said and dropped a duffel bag on my lap.

I unzipped the black duffel. The glittering crown looked back at me, the diamonds sparkling as they caught the light.

The heart-shaped aquamarine was missing.

Chapter 8

I SAT ON the couch in the dark media room, watching the security feed from the camera. Bern had forwarded it to our tv. The Sealight without the jewel rested on the couch to my left. The bloodstained rapier lay across my lap. My whole face was puffy. A large lump had formed on the right side of my forehead. It throbbed. My skin felt hot and ready to burst. I had an absurd feeling that if my lump healed, a pocket of skin would just sag off the side of my face. Google would probably tell me I was crazy, but I didn't care enough to do a search on it. I stopped caring about a lot of things. It had been that kind of a day.

On the screen, the table and chairs where I had interviewed Maria and Lance waited quietly for the victims of Bern's phone spoofing.

Mom walked into the room and flicked the lights on. "Why are you sitting by yourself in the dark . . ." She saw my face, fell silent, and sat on the couch near me. We sat together and watched the empty table.

"I don't want to go to college," I said.

Mom just looked at me.

"There is so much pressure to go to college. It starts from the first day of high school and never lets up. Every grade, every test, every club, every sport, everything matters, and not because you want to do it, but because it might count toward the college scorecard. You're supposed to do great on your SAT, get a scholarship, graduate with honors, and then leave to have this awesome college experience. Winners go on to colleges, losers stay home and work crappy jobs. Well, I'm a loser, Mom. I think you should go to college if there's something you want to do that can't be done without a degree. I don't know what I want to do. I'm not going to waste your money and I'm not going to torture myself just because someone might think that I failed at life because I didn't move halfway across the country to get a degree I don't want."

I braced myself for the crushing disappointment on Mom's face.

"Okay," Mom said.

Okay? What did okay mean?

We sat some more.

"Someone's poisoned Nevada's wedding cake. There is a man whose job it is to impersonate people's relatives for a fee. Bug says the company has a really good medical plan. Also, I got in a sword fight."

"Did you win?" Mom asked.

"I didn't lose, and he cheated." I looked at her. "Also, I have learned how to use my magic to get people to tell me their secrets and then make them forget that they did. I'm like Nevada and Grandma Victoria, except I don't force people. When I violate their minds, I just dangle my magic in front of them and they trip over themselves to tell me everything they know."

I looked back at the screen.

Mom hugged me.

"Are you mad about college?" I asked.

"No. I've done my job. I've raised you to be a good person. You're kind and smart and when you see a wrong, you try to fix it. That's all a parent can hope for. The rest is up to you. It's your life. You have to live it, and I would be a terrible parent if I tried to do it for you. I have no doubt that if you want a formal education in the future, you will get one. Everyone's path is different, Catalina."

"We found the crown under some bushes," I said. "They took the jewel out of it and left the expensive diamonds behind. It doesn't make any sense, does it?"

"It doesn't make sense, because you assume the thief wanted the crown for the money or because they wanted to embarrass the family. Maybe they just wanted the jewel from the start."

Bern walked into the room carrying his laptop. He landed in the recliner. "Did you see the email from Bug about Mikel?"

"I saw." It explained a lot of things.

"Are we ready for this?" Bern asked.

I nodded. Bern typed in a quick sequence. The camera zoomed in slightly, bringing the table into better focus.

"What's going on?" Mom asked.

"Earlier today we sent Lucian a text from Mikel's number telling him to meet in that spot at eight o'clock." I pointed at the tv. "We sent an identical text to Mikel from Lucian. It's seven fifty-five."

"Mom," Arabella called from the depths of the warehouse.

Mom hugged me again, kissed my forehead, and walked out.

Lucian walked into frame. He looked around, clearly impatient.

A minute passed. Another.

Mikel came striding down the path. He hurried to the table and stepped in close to Lucian. They were the same height but where Mikel was thin and awkward, Lucian looked fit and athletic.

"What is it?" Mikel hissed. "I've wired the payment. What the hell do you want from me?"

"I don't want anything from you. You . . ."

"Then stay the hell away from me. There's no more. You're bleeding me dry as it is. Leave me alone."

Mikel took off down the path at a near run.

Lucian looked after him and sneered. There was something very familiar about that sneer. Lucian pulled out his phone and typed something.

"Who is he texting?" I wondered aloud.

"No way to tell," Bern said. "The angle is wrong."

Lucian didn't seem in a hurry to leave. We waited.

A slim figure came down the path and stopped by the table, her chestnut hair spilling over her shoulder.

"Have you lost your mind?" Eva asked.

"I miss you," Lucian said.

What?

"Really? Now, here of all places, with all the family here, you miss me?"

Lucian moved toward her, and she stepped back.

"What you and I did is in the past," Eva said. "It's over. It has to be over."

"It's not really over, is it? Some consequences can't be ignored. Especially when they blunder so badly." He took another step toward her. "Come on, Eva. Let me help you escape this house, if only for an hour or two."

She turned around and dashed down the path. Lucian rolled his eyes and started walking in the direction of the house at a leisurely pace.

"Clearly, this is not Lucian's night," Bern said.

"Can you bring up Lucian's image?" I asked.

Lucian's face filled the screen. He was a very handsome man. Dark hair and a distinctive line of the jaw.

I picked up my phone and dialed Rogan's number. He answered, "Yes."

"Can I have permission to request a DNA test from the Scroll database to determine if someone is a relative of House Rogan?"

"Why?" Rogan asked.

I told him.

"I'll make the call," he said.

I thanked him and hung up.

"Well, that is a hell of a thing," Bern said.

I rubbed my face and wished I hadn't. It hurt. "This is a messed-up family."

"I've got a very nice shot of Isabella collecting money from Elba and restocking her with Oxy," Bern said. "Does that cheer you up?"

"We still don't know who took the Sealight."

"You should rest," Bern said. "You'll feel better in the morning."

"I want to look at some more footage. Maybe there's something I missed."

Bern got up and put the laptop in front of me. "The folders are marked by date. Have fun."

It was past 1:00 a.m., when I watched a gang of kids run down the hallway. Behind them Mrs. Rogan followed in her wheelchair, a happy smile on her face. You would never know she was a dragon. Mia Rosa trailed her, dragging her stuffed unicorn.

I was so tired, I almost missed it. Mom must have heard me laughing like a lunatic, because she came in, confiscated the laptop, and chased me off to bed.

IT WAS FRIDAY, two days after Xavier had headbutted me and the swelling had finally gone down. I had another bruise on my shoulder, because on Thursday morning Arabella saw my face and we had to physically restrain her from jumping into the car and driving to Mountain Rose to "fix Xavier's face so good, his mom wouldn't recognize him." She accidently punched me while swinging her arms, and then she felt bad, and followed me around trying to get me to eat chocolate she bought for me.

Also, on Thursday Nevada called. She had finally closed the Nightingale investigation. House Nightingale was satisfied, and Rogan and my sister were going to celebrate. Arabella and Grandma Frida wanted to know which restaurant they would be going to, and the answer turned out to be Domino's. They had ordered pizza and spent the evening watching bad movies.

Today was the day of the rehearsal dinner. None of the high-ranking guests were coming, so it would be just the two families, Rogan's and ours. The wedding was on Saturday, and everyone involved would be spending the night at Mountain Rose.

I had driven to Rogan's house and met him in his kitchen, while Nevada was getting ready. Rogan was in a hurry, and so he used his magic to do several things at once. I would never get used to the coffee carafe pouring the coffee by itself.

"What's up?" he asked, as the coffee mug landed in his hand.

"I found out some things about your family which you probably should know. They're unpleasant."

"I've known that for years."

"No, I meant the things I found out were unpleasant."

"I knew what you meant," he said. "Why don't you just tell me what's bothering you?"

"I can either expose all those things, or I can tell you and Mrs. Rogan in private. If I do it in public, it will get ugly."

"Are you afraid?" he asked.

"No," I said. "But I don't want you or Mrs. Rogan to be embarrassed or uncomfortable. You're the client. Tell me what you would like me to do."

"Do any of those things compromise or have the potential to compromise the security of the family?" he asked.

"Yes."

Rogan drank his coffee. "I say let's get it all out there. As much as my mother wants to retain her privacy, she would be the first to tell you that potential security issues override that. Do what you need to do."

"Okay." I just hoped he wouldn't regret it.

THE REHEARSAL DINNER took place in the courtyard.

In twenty-four hours everyone was going to be dressed up, so for the rehearsal we went with casual. Tables were set out, covered with white tablecloths. Pitchers of lemonade and iced tea were distributed. Baskets of rolls were placed on the tables, next to simple centerpieces of wildflowers in plain glass vases. Valentina's House Catering had prepared a traditional Texas barbecue, and platters of smoked meats made their way around each table—moist and dry brisket, smoked chicken and turkey, beef and pork ribs, sausage rings with jalapeno kick, followed by bowls of coleslaw, corn on the cob, and baked beans.

I sat at the head table, with Rogan and Nevada, together with Arabella, Bern, Leon, Mom, and Grandma Frida, and Mrs. Rogan. My seat was on Nevada's left, because I was the Maid of Honor. My sister practically glowed.

I felt so bad. I had warned her that some crazy stuff was coming, but I didn't go into specifics. It was either ruin the rehearsal dinner or the wedding. This was the lesser of the two evils.

Mrs. Rogan smiled at me. "It's time, dear."

I got up and walked to the raised porch where Rogan had set up a huge flat-screen tv. To my right stood a lectern covered with a length of blue cloth.

Rogan's entire family was in front of me. My family too. So many people. They were all looking at me. My skin felt too tight. I glanced around the tables, noting the familiar faces. Lucian and June; Maria and Mikel; Markel and Isabella; Iker and Eva, sullen Xavier sandwiched between them; Ane and Lance; Zorion and Teresa . . .

I took a deep breath. I had spent a good hour writing the intro to my speech and trying to sound as adult as I could. "Recently we became aware that the Sealight tiara, which is traditionally worn by the brides of the Ramírez family, has been stolen."

The courtyard went quiet, surprise and concern registering on people's faces. The blue cloth hiding the lectern fell to the floor, revealing a blue pillow with the Sealight on it, its jewel still missing.

"We were able to recover the Sealight and in the process of our investigation, several facts have come to light, which I will now share with you."

I looked at Elba sitting at the table with her parents, Mikel and Maria. Elba grinned at me. *Keep smiling. Let's see if you are still smiling when I'm done.*

I smiled back and looked to the table where Markel and his wife, Isabella, sat. "Isabella Ramírez is buying and selling prescription medication and is using Elba and two other children, not related to the family, to distribute it. Here's the footage of her resupplying Elba and collecting the money."

The flat screen came to life showing Isabella counting off OxyContin pills into the jar and handing it over to Elba.

"The authorities in Bilbao are aware of her activities due to one of the parents of the other children filing a police report."

A copy of the police complaint appeared on the screen. Bug really was a wizard.

The smile fell from Elba's face. Isabella went bright red, then white. Markel stared at her. "Why?"

"Because you have me on an allowance like a child,"

she snapped. "This man rations everything. He wants to know where every euro went. He would ration my tampons if he could."

Maria was glaring at Elba. The next part was going to be even better.

"Maria Ramírez," I said.

Maria jerked in her seat.

"Your husband is not bisexual. He is not having an affair with Lucian. Mikel is running a Ponzi scheme through Ramírez Venture Capital. To date, he has embezzled thirty-four million euros from investors. Lucian de Baldivia became aware of the theft, because his company provides cyber security for Ramírez Capital. He has been blackmailing your husband for the last five months. Here are the financial statements to prove it. They have also been sent to all of your email addresses."

The courtyard exploded. Everyone shouted at once. Ramírez Venture Capital was the family's piggy bank.

"I've made some bad investments!" Mikel yelled over the noise.

"You had no authority to make any investments!" Mattin Ramírez thundered. "You were supposed to sit on your ass and watch the money. That's it. An idiot could have done it."

"I will pay back every euro with interest!" Mikel shouted.

"How?" Ane demanded. "With more fraud?"

"There was no affair?" Maria cried out. "Why do you keep running away from me?"

"Because you drive me insane!" Mikel fired back.

Rogan leaned his elbow on the table and rested his chin on his hand, watching the chaos like it was a Saturday morning cartoon. Mrs. Rogan was rubbing her temples. Nevada leaned back out of her mother-in-law's view and gave me a thumbs-up.

"I want a divorce!" Maria announced.

"I am not done," I announced. "Please let me finish."

"There can't possibly be more," Zorion Ramírez said.

The image on the tv blinked, replaced by Xavier at the fountain. I let his rant roll in all of its glory. When he got to the point of how he would inherit, the courtyard went completely silent. Everyone stared, horrified. The look on Xavier's face was pure hate. I pressed pause on the remote and looked directly at him.

"Xavier, do you know why your plan won't work?"

He cursed at me.

I pressed play. Two images appeared on the screen, side by side. Lucian and Eva. A third image, a document with the Scroll logo on it, popped up under them.

"We have obtained permission from Mattin Ramírez, who is the acting head of your family for the duration of this visit, to test your blood, which you left on my rapier. You do not share DNA with anyone in the Ramírez family. Your DNA profile, however, indicates with a 99.999998 percent certainty that these two people are your parents. You will not inherit, because you are not related to Rogan."

The silence was deafening. Everyone was looking at Lucian and Eva.

Lucian bared his teeth while Xavier shot up to his feet. "It's not true! Mom, tell them it's not true!"

Eva swooned and fainted. Iker stared at her as if he didn't know who she was.

"Almost forgot," I said. I picked up Sealight, stepped off the porch, walked over to the children's table and smiled at Mia Rosa. "May I see Sapphire, please?"

Mia Rosa raised her unicorn up. A bright blue jewel in the shape of a heart glittered in the stuffed toy's forehead, the white fur around it stained with streaks of purple school glue.

"Did you try to bedazzle it?" I asked.

"The bedazzler wasn't big enough," Mia Rosa said. "I glued it."

"I'm sorry, but it's not yours." I plucked the jewel from Sapphire's head and fitted it back into the crown. The Sealight was whole again.

"You should probably give it back to your aunt," I told her.

Mia Rosa, Prime Telekinetic, sighed. The tiara floated from my hands, dodging the guests with surgical precision, and came to rest gently on the table in front of Mrs. Rogan.

Behind me a table fell as Iker Ramírez threw himself at Lucian de Baldivia.

Epilogue

THE WEDDING WAS BEAUTIFUL.

Nevada looked like a princess with the Sealight tiara on her head, while Rogan looked like himself in a tuxedo. The powerful and magically elite of Texas had gathered in full force. The Herald had declared that an invitation to this exclusive wedding was the most coveted in the last ten years. They also snuck a mole into the wedding. I told Rivera to not bust them until after the vows were said. As the woman was gently expelled, her last post on Herald announced that Nevada's lilac bouquet was to die for. Apparently power and wealth trumped the clashing colors.

The wedding ceremony ended, and the reception began. The guest list read like a who's who of Texas Houses. Augustine Montgomery, Best Man, Prime. Linus Duncan, Prime. Lenora Jordan, Prime. House

Harrisson, House Latimer, House Ade-Afefe, House Etterson, House, House, House . . . Even Grandmother Victoria managed to secure a temporary supervised release. She danced with Linus Duncan and had a civil conversation with Grandma Frida, both of which weirded me and Arabella out.

So many rich and powerful people gathered in one spot. Xavier would have loved it. Unfortunately for him and half a dozen other of Rogan's relatives, their invitations had been revoked and they were even now flying back to Europe. Of the west wing, only Zorion and Teresa and Ane and Lance remained. June and her daughters were invited but declined to stay.

In the happy commotion nobody noticed me, Rivera, and several of Rogan's soldiers walking into the kitchen, where the waitstaff and the caterers were preparing and plating the various courses for the reception. Nobody paid me any attention as I walked up to a middle-aged woman with recently bleached blond hair. She was straightening her waiter's uniform.

"Kelly Waller?" I asked.

She glanced up, a flicker of panic in her eyes, but I had already cast my magic lure.

"Give me your gun," I said. And she did. And then she and Jeremy followed me meekly out of the house and into a waiting armored vehicle. So ended the story of Kelly Waller, without fanfare, with a whimper, as she deserved.

Whatever happened to her after this, I didn't feel bad for her at all. Her son, Gavin, was at the wedding and would have eaten the poisoned cake. Her hatred was so strong, she was willing to sacrifice her child to it. I wrote an email to Rogan and Nevada outlining the whole thing. It was my wedding gift to them. They would read it later when they had a chance.

I had watched Nevada and Connor dance under the glittering strands of lights hanging from the trees. They looked like they had stepped out of a fairy tale. Happiness lit my sister's face and it made everything worth it. She took care of us for so long. She deserved to have all the happiness in the world.

They were still dancing, but I was worn-out. I wandered through the house, away from the fading music, until I ended up in Mrs. Rogan's study. She hadn't bothered to lock it. I sat on the window bench and looked outside at the moon.

I felt so tired and empty.

I wanted to cry.

A mechanical whisper made me turn.

"There you are," Mrs. Rogan said. "I've been looking for you."

"I'm sorry. I didn't mean to intrude into your private space."

"You're not intruding. I wanted to thank you for helping me. It was a very heavy burden to put on someone so young. If I had known how difficult it would be, I probably wouldn't have asked you to do it."

"I didn't mean to ruin the relationship between you and some of your family members."

"You didn't ruin anything. You didn't cheat, you didn't steal, and you didn't plot to profit from my son's misfortune. You seem so sad, Catalina. You've done so well. Everyone is proud of you. I thought you would be celebrating."

The words kind of tumbled out on their own. "I don't belong here."

Mrs. Rogan frowned. "Here where? In this house?"

"No. In this space." I wasn't explaining it very well. "Before Nevada met Connor, we all pretended that we were ordinary. Even after she met him, when I had to use my magic, I could still pretend that those were isolated incidents. Nobody knew I was a Prime except for people we trusted. And then we became a House. When I was working on this wedding, I had to use my magic. And it worked. I had tried things that were purely theoretical, and they worked."

"Why is that cause for concern?" Mrs. Rogan frowned.

"Because my magic always came with a price. It was only to be used as a last resort. There was no expectation placed on me. I didn't place any expectations on myself. Now I have learned I can use my magic just like any other Prime. There is no hiding from it now. The next time I'm involved in an investigation for our family business, I will likely use it. Sooner or later, people will realize I'm a Prime and that scares me."

"Because being a Prime puts you in greater danger?" Mrs. Rogan asked.

"No. I know how to be Catalina Baylor, ordinary person. I know what's expected of me. I have no idea how to be a Prime. I don't know what the rules are. I need the rules. They make me feel safe. As long as I followed the rules for using my magic, nobody got hurt." I waved my arms. "All my rules are gone. I don't know how to be. I don't know when other people are breaking the rules and how I'm supposed to react to it when they do. Like this room." I pointed at the bench where I sat and the colorful pillows. "I don't know how to mix these patterns together. If I tried, I have no idea if the result would be tasteful or tacky. I feel like I'm drowning."

I should not have said all that.

Mrs. Rogan leaned back in her chair. "When I left Spain and came here with Connor's father, I felt like I was drowning too. I didn't know anyone. I had no idea how to be a Prime in Texas. I didn't know what was expected of me and I couldn't tell if I was making a fool of myself. But I learned. All those things you have listed can be learned."

"I don't have anybody to teach me."

Mrs. Rogan smiled. "That's not true. You have me. And I have nothing but time. I think we should start with fencing. I suspect there is a lot more to the way you move your sword than pure luck."

**Are you ready for the next installment
in the Hidden Legacy series?
Catalina's story continues in 2019!**
In the meantime, be sure to check out
Nevada's story . . . available now!

BURN FOR ME

Nevada Baylor is faced with the most challenging
case of her detective career. Then she's kidnapped by
Connor "Mad" Rogan, a darkly tempting billionaire
Prime—the highest rank of magic user. Rogan's after the
same target, and the two of them must put aside their
overwhelming attraction and join forces to stay alive.

WHITE HOT

Nevada's new case pits her against the shadowy
forces that almost destroyed the city of Houston
once before, bringing her back into contact with
Rogan. There's no hiding the sparks between
them, and now that the stakes are even higher, and
their foes are unimaginably powerful, Rogan and
Nevada will find that nothing burns like ice . . .

WILDFIRE

Dealing with Rogan and their evolving relationship
is frustrating enough, but Nevada must also navigate
the complex magical world in which she's become a
crucial player. When they're confronted by a new threat
within her own family, can Nevada and Rogan face this
together? Or is their world about to go up in smoke?

About the Author

ILONA ANDREWS is the pseudonym for a husband-and-wife writing team. Ilona is a native-born Russian and Gordon is a former communications sergeant in the US Army. Contrary to popular belief, Gordon was never an intelligence officer with a license to kill, and Ilona was never the mysterious Russian spy who seduced him. They met in college, in English Composition 101, where Ilona got a better grade. (Gordon is still sore about that.) They have coauthored two *New York Times* and *USA Today* bestselling series, the urban fantasy of Kate Daniels and the romantic urban fantasy of The Edge and are working on the next volumes for both. They live in Texas with their two children and many dogs and cats.

Discover great authors, exclusive authors, and more at hc.com.